SUN
CHASERS

尋夢者

Yang, Jwing-Ming
&
Robert J. Woodbine

Cover by Axie Breen

Acknowledgements

The authors would like to express their deep appreciation to Mr. James Norman for his final proof reading of this novel. They would also like to thank the many friends who read and expressed their opinions on the story.

INTRODUCTION

The Communist party in the Soviet Union disintegrated in 1989. All past Eastern European Communist countries, Poland, Romania, Hungary, etc. were set free. The social systems in all these countries were dramatically changed and favored emulating the American democratic system. The entire society was in chaos and disordered. The economic structures collapsed. Daily ordinary life was even harder than before. In one way, the new generation had been given hope for a positive new life. In another way, they had become the victims of this new social chaos. Many people, including countless youths, ran away from their own countries to the western European countries in search of a new life. Unfortunately, they were often either deported or mistreated by the western society because of their illegal immigration status and language differences.

Like many others, 16-year-old Daniel Eraclid, together with two of his best friends, ran away from their mother country, Romania, hoping to find opportunities to live a prosperous life in western European countries. However, like most other refugees, they were abused when they entered these western countries. They struggled to survive in the real and cruel world. After six years of searching for hope, Daniel finally found his opportunity. After he became successful, he established several rescue centers to help refugees and homeless people. He also searched for one of his two friends who ran away with him in the beginning but had become lost.

PREFACE

For the past 30 years, as a result of teaching my seminars, I have traveled to more than 32 countries around the world. Most of the time, I traveled in both eastern and western European countries. From these trips, I saw many of the east European refugees running away from their homes to the western European countries illegally in search of hope and new lives. I also heard many stories of the severe mistreatment and great suffering these refugees experienced by both local governments and the local general public. There were very few people who had placed themselves in these refugees' position to try to understand and help them. Often, if local policemen caught them, the refugees would be sent back to their country of origin. If not, they would be abused, tortured, or placed in slavery by local gangsters or the mafia. In order to survive, many of those young male and female refugees were forced to sacrifice the purity of their heart and soul and use sex as a bargaining token.

One night in Paris around 1993, a few friends took me to the streets where all the shops and restaurants were located. I saw a young man about 17 years old with sloppy clothes kneeing down at the center of the narrow sidewalk. He held a sign in front of him. Through my friends' interpretation, I realized that this young boy was a refugee from Romania who came to Paris in search of hope for a new life. He was begging for food. When I saw him, it reminded me of my childhood during the 1950's. The Taiwanese government was busy preparing for the war to counterattack mainland China at the time. The economy of Taiwan was in dire straits equivalent to or worse than the situation during WWII. I grew up as the second child among nine.

Life was very difficult and relatively hard for almost everyone except those who were rich or government workers.

When I saw this young man on the ground, it was unavoidable that my eyes became teary. Though I had seen many refugees on the street for a few years in Italy, Spain, Germany, and many other countries, my emotions were especially moved by this young man kneeing down. He was so close to me and I could see his facial expression; the expression of begging for mercy and compassion. One of my friends told me that usually these street refugees were already absorbed into the local gangster or Mafia culture in order to survive. Whatever he received from begging, he would not keep the full amount. All of the money belonged to the gangster family. That's how these refugees survived.

Since that experience in Paris, I have had a desire to write a story about these unlucky 'sun chasers' who run after the sun in the west. It seems that it is a hopeless situation, but there is always hope. Through this story, I wish to bring the public's attention to this problem and, hopefully, have them extend hands of love to these refugees. I also wish all the local governments were able to generate a good and kind policy to help them instead of despising them and mistreating them. Though the story of this novel was created based on what I have known or heard, I hope, through this novel, I am able to stimulate readers' compassion and kindness. We in the west should realize how lucky we are and that not all people are as fortunate. Understanding the fate of others less fortunate may help us complain less and appreciate more of what we have already. If we are able to demonstrate some compassion and love, I believe the world will be a more harmonious and peaceful place.

November 17, 2006
New Jersey, USA

I discontinued my writing of this novel after a couple years. The reasons for this were because I realized that, even though I had a good story to tell, I did not have good enough English to express it well. Furthermore, I did not have a western cultural background to write a good western story.

Later, in 2016, I met Dr. Woodbine who was interested in the story and wished to help me complete it. With Dr. Woodbine as a co-author, together, we made this story more idiomatic, vivid, and western like. Without his participation, this book would never have been completed.

October 5th, 2016
Reykjavik, Iceland

HISTORICAL BACKGROUND

Many times, people in Communist countries rose up against the system, but failed. The memory of a few well-known uprisings, such as in Berlin 1953, Budapest 1956, or Prague 1968, were still fresh in people's mind. The Berlin wall was built in 1961 to prevent E. German people from escaping to W. Germany.

Though the Soviet Union could still control their satellites, new policies were chosen in 1984 with the new leader, Mikhail Gorbatshov. In Gorbatshov's reforms, Perestroika and Glasnost should renew the Stalinistic system in the Soviet Union, but not replace the Communist system. These reforms had significant influence on other Communist countries; especially Poland and Hungary. This triggered the foundation of the first free labor union in Communist Poland in 1989. The end of the Communist system had begun. On August 23, 1989, Hungary opened the iron curtain to Austria.

For a few months, thousands of East German tourists took this opportunity to escape to Austria through Hungary. Just in September of 1989, there were more than 13,000 East Germans who escaped via Hungary within 3 days. It was the first mass exodus of East Germans since the erection of the Berlin Wall in 1961. In addition, mass demonstrations against the government and the system in East Germany began at the end of September until November 1989. East Germany's head of state, Erich Honecker, was forced to resign on October 18, 1989. The new government initiated a new law to lift the travel restrictions for East German citizens. On November 9, 1989, the deadly border was opened by East Germans peacefully. This had ended the Berlin Wall.

In Romania, as the result of the military occupation and the agreements of I. V. Stalin and W. Churchill in Moscow (in the autumn of 1944), Romania fell into the Soviet sphere of influence. With Soviet support, the Communists gradually increased their ranks in the government. A pro-communist government headed by Petru Groza took over power in 1946. On June 1946, Marshal Ion Antonescu was executed. On December 30th, 1947, King Michael I was compelled to abdicate; democratic opposition forces were brutally liquidated. After 1948, Romania entered the network of Soviet Satellite countries.

Soviet-style nationalization and collectivization followed the communist take-over. Industrial enterprises, mines, banks, and transport facilities became subject to a planned economy. In 1951, five-year plans were introduced to develop industry and agriculture. But in the 1960s, under the leadership of Gheorghe Gheorghiu-Dej and his successor, Nicolae Ceausescu, the Communist Party of Romania began to implement a foreign policy independent of Soviet goals. Socialist state ownership and central planning fostered the rapid growth of heavy industry and forcibly turned Romania from an agrarian into an urban society. During the 1970s, Ceausescu attempted to modernize the Romanian economy further by investing huge amounts of money borrowed from Western credit institutions. Due to his grandiose development projects, the Romanian people were subjected to a rigorous austerity program in the 1980s since Ceausescu wanted to pay off the country's accumulated foreign debt within a short period. The standards of living plunged considerably as Romania exported much of its food and fuel production. The populace was controlled by the secret police (*Securitate*) and the government, dominated by Ceausescu's family, squandered much of the nation's remaining wealth on megalomaniac constructions and feasts. For nearly 25 years, Ceausescu's regime slowly dragged the Romanians into an economic, social and moral deadlock. All these years were dominated by lies, corruption, terror, violation of human rights, and isolation from the Western world. When communist regimes across

Eastern Europe fell in 1989, Ceausescu resisted the trend and reassessed his unpopular policies. Under these circumstances, the spark of the revolt that was stirred in Timisoara on December 16th, 1989 rapidly spread all over the country and on December 22nd the dictatorship was overthrown owing to the sacrifice of over one thousand lives. When the Romanian army joined the uprising against him, Ceausescu fled. He was arrested by the new provisional government, put on trial, and executed (December 25th, 1989).

1
NEW DREAM

Daniel looked with deep appreciation at the faces in the crowd who came to the charity dinner in Milan to celebrate his finding the sun he had been searching for.

Momentarily, he glimpsed a semi-familiar face in the crowd, but was not sure it was the person he had longed to see. He looked too old and so different. But, from the expression of his eyes and the familiar movements, Daniel knew deep in his heart that it could be him.

This brought Daniel back 9 years previously when he was just 16 years old.

Hope

"Have you heard the news? The Berlin wall was taken down a few months ago!" Jean said.

"I heard, but I thought it was a rumor." Daniel replied with a look of curiosity on his face.

"Come on! Everyone talks about it. Just look at our country, Ceausescu was arrested and executed just 3 months ago, wasn't he?" Jean argued trying to persuade Daniel and Anton.

"I believe that it is true. I heard school teachers talking about it." Anton said.

In this small town of Turda, Romania, located near the western border adjacent to Hungary, news was always a few weeks or sometimes even a few months late. On Tuesday, March 13, 1990, just three months after the uprising against Romanian dictator, Ceausescu, classes were cancelled once again. Many teachers didn't come and almost all of the students had left already once they realized that it would be another free day. All except for Daniel Eraclid, 16 years old, and his two classmates, Jean Aron and Anton Joldea, also 16 years old, who were hanging around in a school classroom and chatting.

A new government was still forming, and the economic situation was worsening since the end of the Communist system. Life was difficult; especially for families with many children. Daniel was the second of 4 children in his family. His brother, Florin, only 18 years old, had already joined the army. He believed this was the best way to survive in the hardship. Daniel's sisters, Danisa and Cristina, were, respectively, 14 and 10 years old.

Like most of the residents in Turda, Daniel's father was a farmer. The harvest was always too little to support the family. This was especially true when Ceausescu was in power. Now that springtime had almost arrived, the situation might be better. It was so difficult the previous winter. There was total social chaos and it seemed nobody was sure what was going on and what would happen in the future. Everyone just hoped the situation would improve when warmer weather arrived.

"Actually, I knew two school teachers, who had already run away from the country. You know, the Hungarian border had already been opened to Austria since last August. Now, we have a chance to go to western countries. I also heard the Berlin Wall had been torn down last November. There is a free path to western countries now." Jean said.

"I think this is the most exciting time for all of us. If we don't take advantage of this opportunity, it may be gone soon. What do you think? I think we should also leave for the west to search for a new life and hope." Jean continued.

"But we don't know those western countries. All we know about them was from TV or what people said. We know they were all rich, but how much chance do we have?" Anton questioned.

"Everything is unknown until you really try it, isn't it?" Jean said.

Daniel kept quiet and listened. Though he also believed that it would be a great chance for them to find a brighter future in western society, he was more cautious. "Can we find a job there? We are only 16 years old. We don't know any of their language except some German and Russian we learned from school." He thought.

"I believe there are probably thousands of people with the same thought. The question is how much chance do we realistically have? It's just like you can see the sun, but you cannot reach it." Daniel said.

"Don't be a coward! Look! We already know there is not much hope here for the next 10, maybe 20 years. I am willing to take a risk to face my destiny." Jean said.

After they talked for a while, they went home. This thought of running away lingered in Daniel's mind. He didn't know if he should run away or stay to help his parents with farming? Springtime was coming, and they would need him; especially since his elder brother was in the army and his two sisters were still young. He believed he had the responsibility and duty to stay.

For dinner, again, there were some potatoes, dried cabbage, and bread. These were left over from last year. It would be another couple of weeks before they would plant anything again. Eating some meat was a luxury for a farmer during this challenging period. Daniel always felt hungry.

After dinner, he sat alone outside of the house thinking, "What do I want for my future? What will be the meaning of my life? Is this the life I want? Should I wait here for the social system to improve or should I go to find a new dream?"

He couldn't sleep. He kept hearing the daytime conversation with his two best friends. The next morning, when he was ready to go to school again, Jean came.

"Hi, Daniel! Let's go to school together."

Daniel took some books and put them into his backpack and left home with him.

"Actually, like yesterday, I don't believe we have school today either. Ya! You know! I heard that Mihai and Vintila had run away two days ago."

"No wonder we have not seen them for a couple days." Daniel said.

"What do you think? Anton and I have decided to run away in a couple days and see our luck in the west. Do you want to join us? We'll have fun and accept the challenge together. If we are together, we can also help each other."

"I don't know. I am still thinking about it. Did you talk to your parents?" Daniel asked.

"Are you kidding? They won't agree with us. You know! All parents are the same. We must keep this a secret."

When they arrived at school, they could see there were not too many students around. There was a note on the wall notifying students that the school was re-organizing and that classes would resume the following week.

They found Anton who had just arrived ten minutes before them. They came to a wooden bench nearby the fence surrounding their school and sat down together. This March weather could be warm, but also cold sometimes. Today was warmer than usual with a mild breeze. They felt good sitting outside talking.

"We must act quick. If we wait too long, our parents will possibly find out our plan." Anton said.

"What's your decision, Daniel? You know. The three of us are always best friends. It will be great if we can experience our lives in the west together." Jean said.

"Let me think some more about it. My parents will need me in a couple of weeks. I feel guilty to run away now. I am the oldest child in the family now and I must help my parents."

"OK! I understand. Anton and I plan to leave Friday morning, the day after tomorrow. We really wish you were able to join us, Daniel. We will meet here at 8 o'clock Friday morning." Jean said.

"Do you have any money? Tell me your plan." Daniel said.

"No! But I believe that we can survive. I'm sure there are plenty of kind people around. We will go to Hungary first. It's only about 160 kilometers from here. From Hungary, we will enter Austria, and then West Germany. I know West Germany is one of the richest countries in the west. Furthermore, we know some German language. We should be able to survive there." Jean replied.

Anton and Jean's families were also farmers. Jean was the youngest child of 5 in his family, 160 cm tall and weighed about 60 kg. He had two brothers and two sisters. His grandpa was nearly 70 and his parents, 48 and 46. His elder sister was married and had two children, a boy and a girl. His second brother was also in the army. Since Jean was the youngest one, he was somewhat spoiled and loved by others. Jean was always optimistic and felt that he was the luckiest boy in the family. He liked to talk and expressed his opinion without hesitation. Of the three friends, unlike Daniel and Anton, he was more active and willing to take adventure or a challenge.

Anton, however, was one of only two children. A family, with only two children, was not common in the village. He had a younger sister, Anna, just 6 years old. Since he was the only boy at home, he was treated preciously in the family. He usually could not bear too much pressure. Like his father, he was shy, polite, and lacked confidence. He had a pair of beautiful and attractive blue eyes that were seldom seen. He was about 165 cm in height and weighed 65 kg.

Among the three, Daniel, a good-looking boy, was the most thoughtful and cautious one. He did not make a decision easily without thinking about it carefully. He was nearly 170 cm tall and 72 kg in weight even though he was just 16 years old. Due to his farm work, he was strong and more muscular compared to Anton and Jean. Though he was quieter, whenever he spoke, he was more convincing and persuasive.

Chasing the Sun

The thought of running away to fulfill a new dream had occupied Daniel's entire mind the whole day on Thursday. Was this a rare opportunity for his future or would this be a disaster? He knew that taking this step could alter his whole life, an unknown future. He tossed around all night analyzing the situation, but without any convincing conclusion. For some unknown reason, the saying, "The child who has never left home will never grow up." came to his thoughts and he made up his mind. He also understood that he could always return if the situation was not good.

He did not bother to go to school that morning. He remembered from the poster at school there would be no classes till next week. He went to the pond nearby; sat there and pondered. He did not have any money. If he did, it might not even last for a couple of days.

That afternoon, his grandma was taking a nap and nobody else was around. He began to pack some clothes and dried food in his backpack and hid it under his bed.

He did not know how to write a letter to comfort his parents; especially his grandma who loved him so much. He simply wrote, "Grandma, Papa, and Mama, I have decided to seek a new life in the west. This is a rare opportunity that I can't miss. I may be successful. Pray for me. Please forgive me. Your love, Daniel."

Next morning, he put the letter under his comforter. He was sure his Mom would find it after he had left. Daniel's mother was 45 years old and had lived in Turda her whole life. She was a kind and compassionate person who devoted herself to raising her children, supporting his father on the farm, and providing a warm home for the entire family including his grandmother.

With teary red eyes and trying to hide his emotions, Daniel said, "Mom! I would like to go to school early to meet my classmates to discuss some homework before classes resume next week." He looked at his Grandma who was sitting at the corner of the living room and he could not speak.

Without any reason to doubt her son, she said, "Come home as early as possible when you finish then. Your dad will need your help to prepare for plowing. You know, spring is coming."

Daniel couldn't answer. Feeling guilty and sorrowful, he left.

When he arrived at school, Jean and Anton had already been there waiting for him anxiously. When they saw him,

"Thank God! We thought you might not be coming." Jean said.

On Friday, March 16, 1990, they began their journey to the west. The backpacks they carried only had some clothing and very little dried food. Nevertheless, they felt free and filled with hope for the future. They believed it would not be too hard to find the sun. They were young and willing to accept any challenge. As they walked, they laughed and talked about their dreams of the future.

"I believe that we will become rich one day. We will have great opportunities to make money in western countries. As long as we are willing to work hard, we should be able to make a lot of money, right?" Jean asked.

"When we send money back to our families in a couple years, all our friends will envy us and know our decision to leave was right." Jean continued.

Anton just listened and did not say a word. He was scared and felt insecure about having left home. Daniel was more cautious. He listened and cheerfully joked with his friends, but deep in his heart, he had a huge question about the future. He was not as optimistic as Jean.

After they had walked for a while, they saw a few farmers on the road with horse carriages filled with the strong and unmistakable smell of manure. Soon, it would the time to condition the soil for plowing. Although it was rare to see cars driven by farmers at that time, they hitchhiked here and there finding themselves sitting along plowing supplies until they finally reached the Hungarian border. They arrived at the city of Oradea about 20 kilometers from the border.

They were surprised that there was no checkpoint or guards at the border when they arrived. The border was wide open. They began to believe that the rumors were true and that a new era was coming. They were excited and entered Hungary without incident.

They needed to reach Debrecen, a city 25 kilometers from the border before nightfall. They knew that they might have a better chance of finding a decent place to sleep their first night. From Debrecen, it would be another 250 kilometers to Budapest, the capital of Hungary.

2
SEARCH FOR THE SUN

An Unknown Future

Arriving late that evening, the place they found to rest was a street corner where the wind blew weakly. Luckily, the evening temperature was still warm. It could have been chilly since spring had not fully arrived. Having no options and feeling tired, they huddled and curled themselves together in the closed doorway of a building and tried to sleep. The nearby street lamp cast a dim light over them. They had never experienced sleeping in the street. This first night, none of them could fall asleep easily. Finally, around 2 AM, they fell asleep. Having walked the whole day, they were exhausted.

Around 5 AM, Daniel was awakened by whimpering he heard somewhere distant in his slumber. Anton was crying.

"Are you OK, Anton?" Daniel asked.

"I really miss home and my family."

He remembered that just a month ago, his family celebrated his 16th birthday. Though food was sparse, somehow his Mom still found a way to bake him a delicious cake; nothing luxurious, but it was filled with love and cheer. He recalled how his Grandma kept joking about how cute he was when he was born.

Anton trembled from sadness and the early morning chill. Without saying a word, Daniel came closer to him and hugged him. He then covered them together with the coat he brought from home in his backpack. Since Daniel was bigger and more than six months older, he always treated Anton like a younger brother.

Daniel thought, "This is only the first night and already we find ourselves sleeping on the street." He felt the first twinge of emotional doubt. Not long after, they fell asleep again. However, they were soon awakened to the sounds of street noise. It was about 7 AM and the street had gotten busier with the arrival of a new day. People were milling about, but nobody seemed to notice them, and no one bothered them.

After getting up and relieving themselves in the alley between two buildings, Daniel found a water spigot from which they used to wash their hands and faces. The water was cold and clean so they each drank from it with their cupped hands, too. Leaving the building where they had slept, they crossed the street and stood eating the dried food they had brought. They tried to conserve as much of it as they could. They knew that the situation in Hungary was almost the same as in Romania--severe poverty and a lack of food. If they stayed in Debrecen too long, their chances of surviving would lessen. They decided to keep moving forward even though they were still very tired. They needed to get to Budapest quickly.

Through hitchhiking and walking, they finally reached Budapest early that evening. They were so happy and proud of themselves. They had journeyed such a long distance to Hungary's capitol and accomplished it in just two days. However, the dried food they brought was quickly disappearing. When they came to a market place, Anton said, "We need to earn some money, otherwise, we will not survive."

"I know that. However, the economic situation here is no different from Romania. We cannot beg on the street. It would not be successful. We must think carefully and set up a plan." Daniel responded.

Jean was lost and could not offer any constructive suggestions. After a minute, Daniel said, "We are farmers and we can work at a local farm. This is the best time since all the farmers need extra help plowing in springtime."

"But it is still early. They will not be busy for at least another two weeks." Anton said with concern.

"I think we might have a chance if we look for them in the farmers' supply stores. They will be there buying what is needed to prepare for a busy spring." Daniel said.

Excited with hope again, Jean said, "That's right! Let's find out where these stores are."

Using their poor German, they asked around in various marketplaces; especially from those vendors selling farm products like milk, cheese, dried vegetable, etc. From their experience, they knew these vendors were the customers of local farmers. Finally, they came upon what appeared to be the biggest food supply vendor in the marketplace.

Humbly, Daniel spoke to the owner. "Madam, we worked on farms in Romania. Do you know how we can find work on a local farm?"

The owner took a look at them and then smiled. She knew these were runaway kids pursuing a dream. She had seen many like them occasionally in the last 3 months. She was happy to see that Communism had finally collapsed. However, society was completely in chaos. Living was not easy. She looked at them with deep compassion. After a couple minutes, she said,

"I will receive a few deliveries from a local farm tomorrow morning. If you come tomorrow morning, you may ask them."

"Thank you very much, madam. You are very kind. We'll come tomorrow morning." Daniel looked at her with a smile and appreciation.

"I know you are runaway kids searching for a new life in the west. I have seen your type before." The storeowner said.

"Yes, madam. My name is Daniel. These are my friends Anton and Jean. We hope to take advantage of this opportunity to create a new future for ourselves." Daniel said.

While she and Daniel were talking, she noticed that Anton and Jean kept looking at food that was on the counter. She knew they were hungry.

Showing her compassion, she said, "I have a son your age. I can't image how sad I would be if he were to run away from home. Please, wait here." She went to the corner of the store near some wooden barrels and shelves. Walking back to the boys, her arms were carrying something. She said,

"You must be hungry. Please take these pickles and bread. It is not much, but it is what I can offer you."

Unable to help himself, Jean stepped forward to hug her with all his might. He was so hungry; especially seeing so much food on the stands.

"Thank you, madam. You are the nicest lady I have ever met." Anton said sincerely and picked up a piece of bread and a pickle. He was so hungry, too.

Daniel looked at her, his eyes turning red. She smiled at him and said,

"Call me Laura. Eat something. I know you are hungry, too; especially at your age, 15 or 16?"

"We are all 16 years old, madam." Daniel replied and also picked up a piece of bread.

While they were eating, Daniel noticed that Laura was busy arranging and moving heavy items around the store. After they had eaten almost all of the bread Laura had offered them, Daniel politely said,

"Madam, If we can help you with anything, please let us know."

"I apologize for not calling you by your first name, but you seem to be the same age as my Mom. It would be disrespectful to do so."

Laura smiled at them and said,

"Naturally, if you can help that would be wonderful. Some of these items are too heavy for me. You know, I am getting old." She laughed.

For the next two hours, the three boys just followed Laura's directions and rearranged the whole shop. After it was done, the store looked much better, organized, and clean.

"Thank you very much, young men. My husband has been so busy doing other things. I am the only one here and we could not afford to hire any help." Laura explained.

"Do you have a place to sleep?" She asked concerned.

"No, madam. We slept in the streets last night." Jean said in a low voice as he looked at her.

"There is a small storage room in the rear of the store. It is tiny but will keep you warm. If you like, you may sleep there tonight." Laura offered.

Laura's kindness and generosity made them feel as warm as if sunbeams were shining on them. This was only the second night of their journey and it seemed there were angels up there to take care of them. They were encouraged by this kind treatment. Though the storage room was small and cramped, it was far better than sleeping outdoors in the street. This night they slept well.

"Wake up, boys." Laura opened the door and woke them up. It was only 6 o'clock in the morning.

"The farmers are here, if you want to talk to them." Laura said.

They cleaned up roughly and came into the shop from the storage room. There were two farmers talking to Laura. It seemed she was discussing Daniel, Anton, and Jean's request with the two men.

One of the farmers looked at the boys as they entered the shop,

"Do you have experience in farming?" He asked.

"Yes, sir. We all grew up farming. Our families are all farmers." Daniel replied.

He asked them a lot of questions; especially about the names of farmer's tools, how to operate and maintain them. Without hesitation, and in poor German, they answered the questions since they all had been working on their family farms.

"OK. I have a job for you, for 10 days. You will have food and a place to sleep. However, I cannot afford to pay you too much." The farmer said. For him, this was the cheapest labor he could get, and he really needed some extra help now.

"No problem, sir. All we need is some money to buy bus tickets to Vienna." Jean said.

After breakfast, they hopped in the farmer's truck and headed to his farm. It took about 50 minutes to arrive. To their surprise, the size of the farm was much bigger than a private one. Usually, under Communism, farmers had only a small piece of land to farm.

After the farmer explained what needed to be done, they began to work. They felt very lucky to have this opportunity. It would provide a period of time to survive since food and lodging was provided. Though the barn was not as comfortable as being in a house, it at least kept them warm and safe.

The farmer had two children, a boy who was 10 and a girl who was only 6. Since the children were still young, it was now obvious the farmer needed helped. Naturally, the farmer worked with them whenever he could. After the ten days of hard work had passed, they had helped the farmer get ready for plowing. Actually, they finished and exceeded the farmer's expectation.

On that tenth day, the farmer invited them to the family dinner to celebrate. This was the first time they ate a meal together with the farmer's family. Dinner was great and included ham and a fresh chicken. They had not enjoyed such a rich meal for a long time. After dinner, the farmer said,

"You have done a great job. Thank you very much. Here is the payment for your work. It is not much, but it is from my heart. You know the economy these days." He gave Daniel an envelope.

Since Daniel was the tallest and strongest one, the farmer assumed he was the leader of the three. Actually, it was true that Daniel had earned most of the respect from the other two. Bowing, Daniel said,

"Thank you very much, sir. We don't know how to thank you." The farmer said,

"I will drive you back to Budapest this afternoon after lunch. I have a delivery to make there. Be ready by then."

When they left the house after dinner and looked in the envelope, they discovered 20,000 Forint (US$70) inside. They knew it was difficult for the farmer to offer them so much money since the economic situation was so bad. An engineer made only about US$60 per month. The boys appreciated the farmer's generosity even more.

With a radiant smile, Daniel told Anton and Jean, "Hey! My friends. I think we have enough money for a bus to Vienna."

Jean said, "It has been so smooth so far. I believe we will have great fortune when we arrive in Vienna. You know, a rich western country."

It was nearly three o'clock in the afternoon when the farmer arrived with them in Budapest. He took them to the bus station where they could purchase their tickets. Each ticket cost US$12. It was March 28, 1990 and they departed at 4:30 PM heading to the new rich world. It would only take about 3 hours to arrive.

When they arrived at Vienna, it was dark already. They still had some money left with which to eat. The farmer also gave them some dried food. Their recent experience gave them hope and they believed their situation would continue getting better. They could make more money in Vienna since Austria was a richer country. The closer they were to West Germany, the more hope they had. Now, all they needed was to save enough money to get train tickets, US$50 per person, to Munich. They were so excited to be in Vienna. Now, more than ever, they felt closer to experiencing that warmth of freedom from the sun they were chasing.

As they expected, it was easier to beg for and receive money in Vienna. Generally speaking, westerners were generous in extending their compassion to refugees fleeing the recently torn down iron curtain. It was much easier for the boys to communicate with others because they spoke German, However, they knew begging was not a good solution for their dilemma; especially because there were many refugees from other eastern countries begging as well.

Life was not as easy as they expected originally. The money they received from begging was just enough for food, nothing else. Everything was so expensive compared with all eastern European countries. They could not afford any hotel. They slept on the streets a few nights. "We should look for the farms again to see if we can make some money." Jean suggested.

However, they could not find farmers as easily as they had in Hungary. Delivery companies delivered all farm products. If they wanted to talk directly to a farmer, they needed to get out of the city itself. Furthermore, they might just waste the time. Later, they learned all the farmers used modern farming tools and only needed a few people for labor. The biggest problem was they were underage and could not legally operate any farming machines. In addition, they were always asked for ID cards that they did not have. They now began realizing the harsh reality that they were just displaced boys in a strange country without any identities or passports.

About 5 months had passed since they left home. Life had become difficult. After a long day of begging, a street corner is where they usually slept. Despite this, one day they decided to write a letter home because they were very homesick. They just wrote that they were OK without explaining what they were doing or experiencing. Naturally, they did not expect a return letter from their families because there was no return address they could use. Even so, it was somehow a comfort to the boys to let their families hear from them.

After a few months of struggling in Vienna, Anton said, "I am confident that the more we move to the west, the better chance we will have. We should go to Munich and seek our luck there."

"But it will cost fifty US dollars to get a train ticket for each of us. Do we have enough?" Daniel asked.

It was a sunny Tuesday morning in the nearly empty park they found themselves in. They sat down in the grass and took out all the money from their pockets they had begged for. They counted a total of nearly US$110. The food was expensive in Vienna. All they ate was bread and butter and, occasionally, some ham or turkey cold cut.

"We still need at least another forty US dollars for 3 tickets." Jean looked at Daniel and Anton.

"Well, let us work harder and save the money. Let's go to the tourist area and see if we have better luck there." Daniel suggested.

They went to beg at the attractive tourist areas. As expected, they earned more compassion from the tourists there since they were on vacation. However, the boys were also closely watched by policemen. In one way, the policemen showed their compassion, however, they had to balance this against securing the safety of tourists. Anton, Jean, and Daniel felt very uneasy whenever police were around; especially because there were increasingly more refugees from other eastern European countries also begging.

Before Christmas had arrived, the number of tourists vacationing had significantly dropped. The boys moved to the malls instead of the streets to beg. Christmas was coming, and people were busy shopping for gifts. The atmosphere was full of the season's joy. Again, the boys benefited from the charity of shoppers. By the end of the year, they had collected an additional US$70.

"We have enough money for train tickets now. Let's go to Munich after the New Year. There are too many travelers now and it's hard to get tickets." Daniel said.

On January 2nd of 1991, they were on the train, Deutsche Bahn, to Munich with renewed hope. They were excited and anxious. They firmly believed that once they arrived in Munich, their chances for survival would improve. They had heard that Germany's government had put forth great effort to help refugees; especially those from East

Germany. If they were lucky, they might acquire an ID card for working and might find decent jobs

New Hope

From Vienna to Munich, it was only about 400 kilometers. When they arrived at Munich's Hauptbahnhof train station, they were overjoyed. As expected, they got through the border without being checked. Having arrived, they now needed a way to make money. Munich's Hauptbahnhof train station is located in the center of Munich and is one of the largest in Germany providing both regional and international service. The station was typically very busy and more so now, during the holidays, it was teeming with travelers coming and going. The boys realized that if they spread themselves throughout the station to help older ladies carry their luggage, they were able to receive some tips as a reward.

After a few days, they realized that they could make good money working as coolies here and there in the station area. They were so happy. However, they knew that, long-term, finding a regular job was the key to living successfully in Germany. They searched for regular jobs while keeping their coolie jobs. The income they had earned from begging was not enough to pay rent for even the cheapest apartment. Most of the time, they slept in the park or street corners. Even though they suffered, they were not discouraged. They helped each other, and their relationships were closer than real bothers.

Unfortunately, during the next couple months, they saw more and more refugees who had escaped from E. Germany, Poland, Czechoslovakia, Hungary, and Romania. There were more than 15 young refugees from other countries and they now, had more competition for the coolie job in the train station. As a result, the money they could make had become less and less. The worst part of it all was that the various refugee groups from these different countries began to fight against each other over potential customers at the train station.

The chance of finding a regular job was slim since they did not have ID cards. Without success, they went to a refugee center to apply for ID cards and jobs. Too many refugees were applying and those from East Germany had a higher priority. It would be a long time to wait. However, they had hope.

While waiting for approval of their ID card applications, the boys realized they must search for other options to make money. They searched for opportunities doing even temporary jobs in Munich's night life, but opportunities had become scarce and more so because they were also competing with each other. Despite this, they continued to share everything they earned. Again, they sent a letter home, without a definite return address, to tell their families they had temporary jobs.

After four months, they got acquainted with another group of three teenaged boys from Czechoslovakia and became good friends. They knew if they helped each other, they might have a better chance to survive. However, they were aware they would be competing with each other searching for jobs. The oldest one in the Czechoslovakia group was 18 years old and named Wilbur. His brother, Henry, was 16 and their friend, Antony, was also 16 years old. They told Daniel and his friends they found a place to sleep more comfortably than on the street or in the park. They found many large sewage pipes just piled up in an empty field near the city's edge. They could stay inside the tube and felt warmer and more comfortable. During the day, they separated and searched for ways to make money and, when night came, they were there together again. There were also other refugees who occupied several pipes at the other end of the pile. The group of six boys did not know who these other refugees were or how many were there. All they saw was some dim light shining from that direction in the evening.

One evening, while they were out in the streets, they heard a TV news report that a Hungarian refugee robbed an old lady. This person was caught and was going to be deported. The boys felt sorry for this refugee and worried that what had happened might trigger a new policy against refugees by the German government. They feared being targeted and caught by German policemen and deported. They now realized they must be careful and tried to avoid policemen. They didn't expect that the situation was worse than what they originally thought.

Influenced by the news report on TV, local Munich gangsters and skinheads began to hunt refugees from Eastern European countries. Those who were caught were beaten up severely. This made every refugee very scared; even more scared than being caught by policemen. The worst part of this was these skinheads could always find the places where refugees were hiding and sleeping. They heard some refugees talking about this. Skinheads called this "hunting." The refugees were treated like animals, hunted, beaten, or tortured. When the news began to spread about this, more and more refugees ran away from the cities. As a result, there were fewer and fewer refugees in the city. That meant the chance they could be caught was higher and higher.

"I think we should move out of the city to avoid skinheads." Daniel suggested when they were together one night.

"But the chance of earning money will lessen if we don't stay in the city, though." Anton replied.

"I am so scared. I think we should leave Munich and go somewhere else." Jean said.

"Unless we leave Germany to go to another country, it does not matter where we go because there are always skinheads in here. The problem we have is that we don't know any other languages besides German and Russian." Daniel said.

"I think we should go south; especially since the weather will be getting colder in November. Italy is warmer, and I heard people are more generous and kinder." Daniel suggested.

"I thought once we were in West Germany, we would be able to settle down. I think we should go home. I miss home." Jean said with tears.

Hearing Jean say this made Anton sad. He was somewhat regretful that they ran away from home. But he felt so ashamed to return home without reaching the goal.

"I cannot go home though I miss it so much. All my relatives and friends will laugh at me. I need to show them our decision was right." Anton said with red eyes.

They discussed and argued about this but could not come to a decision that satisfied everyone.

One night, when they had gotten together at the corner of a department store to prepare to go back to their sewage tubes, Daniel saw the boy, Henry, was being chased by eight skinheads about 50 yards away. Fearfully, Daniel and the others quickly hid themselves in the darkness near the building. When Daniel looked around, he saw Henry's brother, Wilbur, and Anthony were hidden at the corner of another building. They all just looked at how Henry was caught and pushed down to the ground by the skinheads. They were afraid to come out and do something since there were eight skinheads and all extremely violent.

The skinheads punched and kicked Henry while he was on the ground. Henry cried out in pain and begged them to stop, but that only seemed to encourage them more. They laughed, cursed, and spit on Henry. "This is our country you immigrant bastard. Go back to wherever you worthless scum came from." After ten interminable minutes, the skinheads left and ran through the streets jubilantly. Henry was on the ground motionless. Now, feeling safe, Wilbur, Anthony, Daniel and two of his friends rushed to Henry to see what his condition was. When they saw Henry was unconscious and his body was covered with blood, their bodies trembled uncontrollably, and their eyes were filled with tears; especially Wilbur. Wilbur was so angry and sad. He felt so guilty and ashamed that he couldn't protect his brother. They all knew that if any one of them had encountered the skinheads, he would have experienced the same unfortunate mistreatment. Wilbur just hugged his brother's body with tears and kept calling out his name aloud. He felt that it was his fault that he took his brother away from home in search of the sun. Daniel, Anton, and Jean just looked at them and did not know what to say to comfort Wilbur.

After a moment,

"I am very sorry, Wilbur. I hope Henry is OK." Daniel finally expressed his feeling while Anton and Jean were still trembling.

10 minutes afterwards, they heard the distant sirens from police cars. It seemed someone had called the police and reported the event. Looking up at them from the ground where he sat embracing Henry, Wilbur said,

"Make your decision quickly now. Go home or run." Wilbur looked at them decisively. He had decided to stay with his brother hoping the policemen would be able to save his brother from any serious injury. He knew that choice meant they would be deported even if his brother were saved.

When they heard the police cars get closer and closer, Daniel, Anton, and Jean immediately left and hid themselves again. Peering out from the darkness discretely to see how things unfolded they saw policemen arrive and come out of their cars to help Wilbur and Henry. Several minutes later, an ambulance arrived and took them and Antony away. After that day, they were never seen again. Daniel and his friends all knew that they could not stay there anymore. If they did, skinheads would certainly return and give them trouble. Apparently, the skinheads knew where they hid and slept. Whenever the boys thought of Henry, they became very scared.

Five months had passed since they arrived in Munich. Winter was coming, and the weather got colder and colder. Even though they were able to stay warmer by sleeping in sewage tubes, they were also terrified knowing they could be found and hunted by skinheads at any moment.

A few days before Christmas, the three of them felt so hopeless and insecure. They started a fire in the tube to keep warm and discussed their future. Jean's eyes were filling with tears.

"I want to go home. I miss home so much, and I am so scared." Jean said.

"I think we should all go south and stay together." Anton proposed.

"It is not a good idea to remain together as a group anymore. People are afraid we might rob them; especially after what's being said on TV news. It is easier to earn compassion from a stranger if you are by yourself." Daniel said.

"I know one thing for sure. As long as we stay in Munich, or any place in Germany, we have a greater chance of being caught by skinheads and beaten. We can't stay in Germany anymore." Daniel said.

"But we still have the chance to acquire ID cards." Anton said.

"It has been a few months now. Let's check the refugee center tomorrow and see what they say?" Daniel replied.

They all agreed and the following day went to the refugee center to know if their ID cards had been issued. Unfortunately, they were still on the waiting list. East German immigrants had the higher priority. Getting an ID card soon seemed very unlikely.

That evening, Jean woke up at midnight to relieve himself. When he stepped out of the sewage tube, he saw a few flashlights heading toward their tubes very quickly. Since Henry's attack by the skinheads, he had already had several nights of nightmares. Now, the reality was there. It was obvious that skinheads had finally decided to intrude their nest.

"Wake up, wake up! Skinheads are here!" His voice and body were trembling. He shouted nearly crying.

Daniel and Anton woke up abruptly, and in a few seconds they grabbed their backpacks quickly and crawled out of the end of the tube and away from them. While they were crawling away, they saw that the end of the sewage pipe pile was surrounded.

As they kept crawling farther and farther away, they could hear the shouting and crying of those left behind at the same time. They knew some of the other group was caught. They dared not stay to see what happened. After they had crawled away for some distance,

"Jean, thank you. Without your warning, we might also have been caught." Anton said with a trembling voice.

"Let's get away from here. We cannot stay here anymore." Daniel said.

They did not sleep the whole night and went to a corner of an old building.

"We cannot stay together as a group. We can be spotted easily by the skinheads." Daniel suggested.

Jean was crying and could not stop. He was so scared and sad. Anton just kept quiet without saying a word. When the morning came, they decided to separate and continue to search for the sun each in their own way. They separated on December 20th, 1991. After that day, it would be many years later before Daniel would see them again.

Separation

To avoid skinheads, Daniel went to the east side of the city and hoped no ruthless skinheads were around there. He then decided to go to Geneva, Switzerland because he believed he might have a better chance for his future since German was a common language there. Furthermore, Switzerland was one of the richest cities in west Europe.

However, it would cost about 80 Swiss francs (US$55) for a train a ticket. It would take about 8 hours to get there. He needed to find enough money to buy a ticket. After 10 days of begging, offering help here and there, and his old savings, Daniel had saved enough money for a ticket. On January 2nd, after 8 hours of travel, Daniel arrived in Geneva.

Not too long after arriving, Daniel discovered that, though people in Switzerland are somewhat different from those in Germany, they were still conservative. He did not receive too much money begging in the streets. It was difficult for him to find some temporary job as well. Now, he felt lonely having separated from his two best friends. "I must be strong. I need patience. I will find my sun someday." He kept comforting himself with those thoughts, but deep in his heart, a huge question mark remained.

Now, he was 17 years old and his facial hair grew into a beard and mustache. He looked older than his age; especially wearing sloppy and dirty clothes. The weather was cold now. To keep himself warm; especially at night, all he could do was to hide at some street corner tucked away from the elements. He began to search for food in garbage cans on the street because he had no money. Life was hard in this winter. A couple of months passed without any change.

One day in March, the weather was strangely warm. Walking by a shop window, Daniel looked and saw his image and was shocked to see the reflection of an old man. But he was only 17 years old. After going into a store to buy a razor and soap, he walked outside to the back of the store and found a faucet. Using the semi-freezing water, he completely shaved off his beard and mustache. It was amazingly warm, nearly 20 degree centigrade for this time in March. Taking full advantage of the warm temperature, he took his outer layer of clothes off and washed them. He also cleaned his face, arms, and feet. Now, he looked like a 17-year-old, handsome young man again.

There were more people out in the streets today because of the warm weather. He came to a busy street and hoped to beg for money for some food. He was surprised that he had not gotten sick since he had been eating unhealthily. He believed it must be because of his strong will and spirit searching for the sun which had kept him going. Though he also saw many other run-away people from East European countries on the street, he did not greet them since they were all his competitors.

He knew that if he went south to countries like Italy or Spain, he might have a better chance to prosper. However, he did not have much money and could not afford to buy a train ticket.

One day, after nearly 3 hours of begging, he was tired and sat down on a bench on the sidewalk. He thought of his past, present, and possible future. He deeply missed his friends, Jean and Anton. He did not know what had happened to them. While he was thinking, a gentleman about forty years old, sat next to him.

"Hi, young man, where are you from?" The gentleman asked. From Daniel's clothes, he could see that he was one of the refugees from one of the East European countries.

"Romania, sir." Daniel replied. When he paid attention to this gentleman, he could see that he was an elegant businessman.

"Is it hard to survive having left home?" The man asked.

"Yes, sir. But I will find the way. I hope to find a better future and life in the west." Daniel said.

"Are you hungry?"

"Yes, sir, I'm always hungry; especially because I am only 17 years old and still growing." Daniel replied.

"Come! Come! Let me treat you a dinner." The man said.

Much to Daniel's surprise, he was invited to have dinner by a stranger. He felt he was in heaven since he was desperately hungry, had no money and instead of finding food from garbage cans, would have a nice dinner.

"But, you don't know me, sir. You are so kind." Daniel replied and felt somewhat embarrassed.

"No problem. My name is Samuel. What is your name, young man?" Samuel asked.

"Daniel, sir." For a moment, Daniel felt strange, shy, and embarrassed. "Why is this gentleman interested in me?" He wondered.

They went to a restaurant across the street. After sitting down, Samuel ordered a fish dinner and Daniel ordered steak. It had been a long time since he ate a steak dinner. This was the best meal Daniel had had for the past 15 months. He enjoyed it so much but was curious what it was Samuel wanted from him. After dinner, they ordered some coffee and pies.

"I felt lonely. Do you want to keep me company tonight?" Finally, Samuel asked with hesitation.

Daniel could sense that Samuel implied having sex with him. His face turned flushed. He had never had sex with anyone before, female or male. Confused, he did not know how to reply and hesitated for a long time.

As he faced this gentleman who had been kind to him and who was not bad looking, Daniel could not even imagine what sex would be like with Samuel? Furthermore, he needed money urgently. Daniel kept his head down and hesitated to look directly into Samuel's eyes.

"It will be OK. I won't hurt you. I will also pay you. I think this may help your situation now." Samuel said.

After several moments of hesitation, Daniel finally nodded his head in agreement. Samuel hailed a taxi and, after driving through the city 20 minutes or so, they came to an apartment building. Daniel had never come to this area. However, from the building and the surrounding environment, he knew it was a high-class area. Samuel took him to the second floor where his apartment was and opened the door. It was a single bedroom apartment with a small kitchen and living room with two windows facing the street. One of the walls was full of books and there was a comfortable chair there with a small desk and floor lamp hovering over an open text. There were two bathrooms, one in the master bedroom and another smaller one at the end of the short hallway separated by the kitchen. The apartment was a little messy but was nice and comfortable. It seemed Samuel lived alone.

"Daniel. The bathroom is at the end of the hall. Please, go take a shower and wash yourself clean. There is a towel inside behind the door. I will take a shower in my bedroom." Samuel said. He could not hide his excitement.

Despite his uneasiness, this was a rare chance that Daniel had to be able to take a warm shower and in such a place. He enjoyed being in the shower so much. He washed and again washed. He didn't know when he would have another chance to enjoy this again. After about 30 minutes, he got out of the shower. He stepped out of the bathroom wearing a white nightgown that was hanging on the bathroom wall and entered the living room. After his shower, Daniel looked so clean and attractive.

He discovered Samuel sitting in the living room also wearing a nightgown waiting for him anxiously. "Great! You look so different now, like a prince." Samuel joked.

"I've never felt so great and clean in this last year." Daniel replied with a smile. Suddenly, Daniel realized that he had not had a smile on his face for a long time. Though he had never experienced sex his whole life, he believed he was mature enough to try it for the first time.

Samuel stood up from the sofa and walked toward Daniel. He pulled gently Daniel toward him with both hands and gave him a soft and passionate kiss on Daniel's lips. Daniel instinctively felt so uneasy with this; especially kissing with a man. However, he did not resist or reject it either. He knew he needed the money to travel to Italy. This is the work, he kept telling himself as Samuel's lips and arms seemed to envelope him like a blanket.

"Come!" Samuel said and led him to his bedroom.

Since Daniel had never had any previous sexual experience, he just followed what Samuel wanted to do. At first, it felt acutely awkward, but after 10 minutes or so, he learned to coordinate his movements.

He experienced a strange mix of feelings; though embarrassed, he somewhat enjoyed it. He had never penetrated anyone and even though he had masturbated alone, it was different to experience an orgasm with another person.

After they finished having sex, Samuel was satisfied and sat up next to Daniel on the bed. As promised, Samuel did not hurt Daniel, but he did not provide him with a condom either.

"You may sleep on my sofa tonight. There are some blankets there. But you have to leave early tomorrow morning. Sorry about having to ask you to go so early. I need to go to work at 7 AM. In the kitchen, there is some food in the refrigerator. You may eat some for your breakfast tomorrow morning." Samuel explained.

Daniel slept soundly even though it was on a sofa. It certainly was much better than sleeping in the street. When Daniel woke up the next morning at 6 AM, Samuel was still sleeping. He entered the kitchen and found some food and heated up some water. When he had just finished, Samuel stepped in the kitchen.

"Great! You have already had breakfast. I usually don't eat breakfast at home." I will eat something near where I work. Remember, I need to leave at 7 o'clock." Samuel said.

Samuel left the kitchen. Daniel wondered if he would get paid before he left. He sincerely hoped so since he needed the money so badly. He returned to the living room and sat on sofa where he had slept. Five minutes later, Samuel came into the living room dressed nicely for work. He gave Daniel an envelope. Daniel guessed it was the money Samuel promised him and he took it.

"Thank you, sir."

Both of them left the apartment together and said goodbye to each other. It was not quite busy with many people walking about and the sun was shining brightly this time of the day. When Daniel walked to a corner where no one was around, he took a peek inside the envelope and found there were two hundred Swiss francs inside. With this money, he could afford to eat nicely for a few weeks. To buy a train ticket to Milan, Italy, he would need more money.

From this experience, he realized that he could make more money easily through selling sex. Though that was not what he wanted, it was a logical and practical choice for making money. He began to wander around in busy night streets; especially during warm days. Surprisingly, he received two other sex jobs, one with a lady and one more time with Samuel. Now, he had earned enough money to go to Milan.

3
SURVIVING

Gangsters

On July 1st, 1991, he took a train from Geneva, Switzerland to Milan, Italy. It cost him only $35 Swiss francs for the nearly 4 hours' trip. Other than paying for the ticket, he still had about US$200 left. This would be a lot of money in Romania, but it would not be much in west European countries.

He believed that he might have a better chance finding a job and surviving in Italy. As he had previously heard, Italians were more open minded and not as conservative as Germans. Furthermore, it would be warmer in Italy than Germany or Switzerland; especially in wintertime. At least there were no skinheads in Italy. When he arrived at this new place, it was nearly 5 PM. It was Monday and the Milan train station, Milano Centrale, was very busy. Once again, he tried to see if he could help some people to carry their luggage and earn some income this way. He had only about $290 Swiss francs in his pocket. After he exchanged this into Italian lira, it was 31,000 lire. He knew he must be frugal with his spending. Although it seemed like a lot, Daniel didn't know this new environment and what it would take to survive in Milan.

Though he received some money here and there helping people by carrying their luggage and through begging, he soon realized the competition was high with the many other eastern European refugees doing the same as he. In just a day or so, he began to understand that all of the beggars working in the Milan train station belonged to a powerful mafia group, Camorra. To avoid the trouble, he knew he couldn't stay there. The scene of that Czechoslovakia boy, Henry, being beaten by skinheads in W. Germany was still fresh in his mind. Daniel knew that he had only two choices: keep himself away from their territory or join them and became a gang member. "I am searching for the sun. I cannot join the gangs. Doing so will be the end of my dream." He thought.

Later, he realized that the entire Milan area was divided into a few different territories which were controlled by different gangs. He learned that he had to move from one place to another every three days to avoid trouble. The living was hard; especially since he also had to avoid policemen's attention. Throughout this, he kept asking any store and different places for a job. However, due to the language barrier and not having an ID card, he was always rejected. Within a few weeks, he again found himself searching for food to eat in the garbage dumpsters. Doing this saved him money since he could always find some thrown away leftover food in the market places. He knew that eating these foods was not healthy and might also make him seriously ill. Daniel felt he had no choice.

One day, he came to a residential area where there were some expensive apartments. He knew that, usually, there were no gangsters in these elegant, high society areas. Occasionally, he was able to receive some charity there. When he saw an old lady step out of her car with a few bags of grocery, he stepped forward and tried to use his poor Italian he learned in the last weeks.

"May I help you, madam?"

The lady looked at him with curiously. Before she said anything, one of the bags began to fall from her hands. Daniel immediately used his hands to catch it. The lady knew if he hadn't caught the bag, the groceries would be all over the ground.

"OK! You can help me carry them into my apartment."

Though Daniel could not understand everything she said, he could feel that she wanted his help. He took over another bag from the lady, so he had two bags in his two hands. The lady carried one by herself. After they entered the apartment, Daniel helped her put her groceries on the kitchen table. Daniel bowed to her and was ready to leave. This surprised the lady since she thought Daniel was expecting some cash reward.

"Wait a minute! Have some cookies." The lady took some cookies from a kitchen cabinet and gave then to Daniel. He smiled and bowed to her and accepted the cookies. Before Daniel left, she said

"Young man, maybe you can help me some other things. I have a few heavy pieces of furniture that I need to move around. They are too heavy for me." The lady talked with her hand postures. Daniel could catch what she meant.

"Si! Signora." He said and followed the lady to her living room.

Actually, the lady wanted to re-arrange her entire living room. The location of the TV and furniture were not in the right place; there was too much light from the apartment window which reflected on the TV screen. Daniel helped her change the TV's position and reorganize the entire set up of the living room until the lady was satisfied. It took him nearly two hours to complete the job.

"Grazie! Young man." She said. She went into her bedroom and came out with some money. She gave Daniel 20,000 lire, equivalent to US$14.

Daniel was very happy since his money was running low. When he was helping the lady to reorganize the living room, from glancing in the mirror, Daniel realized how long and thick his hair, beard and mustache had grown. He knew that with this kind of appearance, he wouldn't be able to find any job or even beg successfully for money. He would just scare people away. He knew he must look clean and neat. Though his clothes were old, they must look clean. He went to a store and bought a shaver, tooth brush, toothpaste, and soap. Sunday afternoon, when it was warm, he went to a warehouse where there was a faucet. Since it was Sunday, there was nobody around. He washed some of his clothes and used the window's reflection to shorten his hair, brush his teeth, and shave. Now, he looked better. After all of this, he brought his wet clothes to a park and allowed the breeze and sun to dry his clothes. While sitting on the bench in the park, he asked himself,

"Should I stay here, or should I go somewhere else?" "But, if I decide to go somewhere else, where should I go? I don't have enough money to continue traveling." He knew that since there were so many gangster groups in Milan, it would be hard for him to survive unless he joined one of those groups. He also knew that, once he joined, he would lose his freedom forever.

About six o'clock in the evening, his clothes were dried. It had surely been a hot day. He decided to go to another new area where there was a night market to see if he could find a job.

While he was wandering through the night market, he noticed that a middle-aged lady kept looking at him. She was dressed modestly, but there was something alluring about her eyes and the turn of her lips when she smiled. He was curious and went to her.

"May I help you, Signora?" Daniel asked. Daniel was hoping to get a helping job to earn some income.

"Yes, young man. I am Alessandra. What is your name?" The lady asked.

"Daniel, Signora."

"I just wonder; would you mind spending the night with me?" The lady looked at him with her intriguing smile.

Now, Daniel realized that she was looking for a sex partner. From his recent experiences selling his body for sex, he knew he would receive a handsome reward like the previous few times.

He nodded his head affirmatively with embarrassment on his face. After all, he had just turned 18 years old.

He followed the lady to her home, a townhouse-like residence, two blocks away from the night market. After entering the door, Alessandra looked for a towel from a closet and gave it to Daniel.

"There is a bathroom, two doors down on the right. Please, clean yourself and wait for me in the living room. I will take a shower as well." Alessandra said with a kind smile.

Daniel went into the bathroom which was nice and clean and had different shampoo and soaps on the counter by the small sink. Behind the mirror in the medicine cabinet, he found new toothbrushes, toothpaste, and a pair of scissors. He still had the shaving tools in his backpack he had bought but decided to use Alessandra's instead. He took a long warm shower and enjoyed the moment. Afterwards, he shaved and cut his hair short with the pair of scissors. Now, he really cleaned himself completely. He felt so good. Though he was only 18 and skinnier than before, Daniel felt like a handsome young man again.

When he entered the living room, Alessandra looked at him with a smile and said,

"You really look nice and clean." From her delightful expression, it seemed she was pleased she had found herself a quality sex partner. She handed Daniel a pack of condoms. She knew, from her experience, that street people might carry sexual diseases. Daniel understood why she was cautious and believed that it was the best for both of them. He had never used condoms before. He was so lucky that he did not get infected from the previous sexual encounters.

Because Daniel did not have much experience with sex, he just followed what Alessandra's demands were, just as he had done with others. He felt that he was just like a sex slave trying to satisfy his master's wish. However, Alessandra was an experienced lover and taught Daniel many skills that would make any sex partner feel he was in heaven. Unlike his past experiences, both Daniel and Alessandra enjoyed each other very much. Even though he was still a neophyte at sex, this night with Alessandra marked a change in him. Strangely, he felt somehow wiser. After they had finished having sex, Alessandra said,

"Daniel, please sleep in the next room. I like to sleep alone."

"No problem, Signora" Actually, Daniel also needed to rest and looked forward to a nice, deep sleep. He entered the next room. Everything was really clean and organized. The bed had clean sheets, pillowcase, and very comfortable blanket. Daniel quickly got in the bed and drifted off into a quite slumber.

The next morning, Daniel woke up early. He went to the bathroom to take another shower. He did not know when the next time would be he might enjoy this kind of luxury.

After his shower, Alessandra was still sleeping. Daniel went to the kitchen and found something to eat. He found an espresso machine on the counter and tried to make some. From watching coffee shops make espresso at the train station, he had an idea of how it worked. As he was beginning to do so, Alessandra stepped in the kitchen.

"You must be hungry." Alessandra looked at him with her wary smile. "Let me fix some breakfast for you."

Alessandra took some milk and eggs out of the refrigerator and began to cook while Daniel was preparing the espresso. They sat together on a small dining table next to the kitchen 20 minutes later to eat.

"I enjoyed last night very much, Daniel. Though it's obvious you did not have too much experience, you listen well, are attentive and gentle, and served my needs well. I felt like a queen last night. Thank you." Alessandra was definitely happy about her experience with Daniel.

"Thank you, Alessandra. I enjoyed it very much as well." Daniel told the truth. He did enjoy the whole experience with Alessandra.

After they ate breakfast, Alessandra went to her room and returned with 100,000 lire. This was nearly US$140 and would help him last for a couple weeks, he thought. Alessandra placed the money in an envelope for Daniel and sweetly kissed him on his cheek. It was time for Daniel to leave and after getting dressed, she embraced him and escorted him to the door. He left Alessandra's apartment at about 9 that morning and walked outside to a Sun that was shining brightly.

In the ensuing days afterwards, Daniel hoped Alessandra wanted to see him again. He wanted to see her, too, as much for the lovemaking as for the money. But, Alessandra never appeared in the familiar market place for nearly two weeks. His money was running low very quickly. He decided to buy a train ticket to Rome. The ticket cost him about 7,000 lire (US$11.00). He left Milan to Rome on October 15th, 1992.

When he arrived in Rome, he was so excited. From books he had read and stories he was told, he knew a lot about Italian history. "This is the city with tourists from all over the world. All of the famous tourist attractions such as the Sistine Chapel with its world-famous ceiling fresco, the Vatican Museums, the Colosseum, etc. are all good spots for earning some money." He thought and sincerely hoped.

He began to move around and beg for money. Not too long after, he realized that it was a very bad idea since there were so many refugees from other countries begging on the street. Making it worse was that there were so many pickpockets around targeting tourists. Signs were everywhere warning tourists to be careful about pickpockets. From his dress and look, he could be recognized easily as a refugee and suspected that he might be one of pickpockets. He noticed that people were alert to his presence. Earning by begging was not as easy as he had thought it would be.

After only one week of his arrival in Rome, he saw at least 10 young refugees taken, handcuffed, and put into three police vans at the Colosseum. To avoid being seen and possibly arrested too, Daniel hid beside a building at the corner near the scene and watched. After the police vans left, he came out and began to realize that Rome might not be a good place to be either. There was too much attention being given to refugees by policemen.

Daniel decided to go further south to Naples. Unlike Rome, it was a business port and not a heavy tourist city. He hoped he might have better luck there. He still had just enough cash to buy a train ticket. On November 20th, he left Rome to go to Naples.

When he arrived at the Naples train station, Napoli Centrale, it was nearly 8 PM. He was very hungry. In fact, he was always hungry now. Unfortunately, he did not have much money left to buy anything to eat.

He wandered through the station trying to find something to eat. It was getting late and there were fewer and fewer people about and the shops were closing one by one. Suddenly, he saw a boy with a lady passing by him. The boy threw a bag in the garbage. After they had walked away, Daniel hoped he could find some food in the bag. Without attracting attention to himself, he opened the garbage can. All he found was an empty can and a bottle. However, he saw there was another bag underneath. Excited, he took it out and quickly walked to a corner where the lights were dim, and no one was around. When he opened the bag, there was some leftover food inside. He did not know how long the food had been in there, especially during this hot summer time. However, Daniel did not care and began to voraciously eat the food he had found. This at least satisfied some of his hunger for the moment.

He walked on the streets for a while looking for a place to sleep for the night. He was feeling very tired and now did not know what his future was going to be. He missed his family, he missed Romania, and he missed his grandma especially. He was sad, and the tears rushed down his cheeks. Finally, he found a hidden alley where he could hide and sleep safely for the night.

About one o'clock in the morning, Daniel was suddenly awakened from a deep sleep with painful stomach cramps. Within thirty minutes afterwards, he urgently had to find a hidden place where he could defecate. He was experiencing a serious bout of explosive diarrhea which left him trembling and feeling cold. An hour later, he began to throw up. Between bouts of diarrhea and episodes of vomiting, Daniel was awake the whole night. In addition to feeling very weak, he felt hot and thought "I think I have a fever." Without money, however, he felt helpless. He could not see a doctor or even buy medicine from a pharmacy. This was the first time he had gotten sick since he ran away. He was extremely weak and knew that without help or medicine, he might die. He came out of the alley and found a corner where he could sit to wait for the sun to come up. He hoped the radiant light from the rising sun would warm him up.

Instead of bright sunshine, it began to rain around 7 AM. He was disappointed and sad. Though he was sick and weak, his mind was still clear. Around 11 AM, he simply sat there and watched people come and go hoping his situation would improve later. While sitting there, a man stepping out of the nearby store spotted Daniel. Their eyes met, and the stranger sensed that Daniel was asking for help.

"Are you OK?" The gentleman asked.

"Signor. I am sick." Daniel replied.

When the gentleman touched Daniel's forehead with his right hand, he felt it was very hot and assumed Daniel had a fever. He knew that Daniel was pretty sick and really needed help.

"Come with me. Let's see if I can find some medicine in my apartment." He said.

Daniel looked at him with sincere appreciation. Though he was sick, he still had his cute and boyish look. Coupled with his immediate need for help, he genuinely touched people around him who readily offered Daniel mercy and kindness.

"Thank you, Signor. My name is Daniel." Daniel introduced himself with a weak voice.

"My name is Alberto. My apartment is only a few blocks from here." Alberto helped Daniel stand up. They walked slowly and took nearly 30 minutes to finally come to an apartment on a side street. Alberto opened the door to his apartment on the ground floor and they went in.

"Take a warm shower first and you will feel better, Daniel. The towel is in the top drawer of the cabinet in the bathroom." Alberto pointed his finger to a door on the left a few feet away from the kitchen down a narrow hallway.

It was a tiny and quite modest single bedroom apartment. In fact, it was a little messy with newspapers on the floor and dust accumulated on the lampshades. Daniel could tell Alberto lived there alone.

After showering, Daniel slowly walked into the living room and saw Alberto there with some medicine on the table in front of the couch.

"Take these pills. It will lower your fever and stop your diarrhea. But before you take it, you must eat some crackers, so your stomach isn't completely empty." Alberto said.

With obvious appreciation, Daniel looked at Alberto and took several crackers with water and then swallowed the pills. He needed to trust someone in this situation as he needed to recover quickly from this illness.

When Daniel sat down, Alberto shared that he originally came from northern Italy to Naples to find work. His parents were farmers and he did not want to be a farmer like them. He came to Naples in search of his own dream. He had a job, but it did not pay much. Daniel felt that Alberto was a very nice and kind man. Alberto was only 5 years older.

"I need to go to work now. I am working in a grocery store and I must be there by 11 AM. Please take a nap on my couch and rest. I will be back around 7 PM. If you are hungry, there is some food in the refrigerator in the kitchen. Please eat as much as you like, but don't overdo it as you are still recovering." After that, Alberto left.

Alone in Alberto's apartment, Daniel felt that he was so lucky. It seemed there was an angel up there taking care of him. Without Alberto's help, he did not know how he would have passed this crisis. He did not feel hungry, just weak. However, after a few hours had passed, he realized his temperature dropped and the diarrhea had stopped. He no longer felt like vomiting anymore. Although his abdomen was tender and sore, he felt much better.

Around 6 o'clock that evening, he felt hungry though still tired and weak. He went into the kitchen and found some bread. From experience with his Mom, Daniel knew he should not eat anything greasy because it would bring his diarrhea back. He just ate a couple of pieces of bread and drank warm water. He needed to baby-sit his stomach carefully for the next couple of days.

Around 6:50 PM, Alberto returned with a bag of food. Daniel stood up quickly to help him with a smile. This was the first smile Daniel had had in the last few days. Alberto smiled back.

"You look much better now. But you still have to be careful about what you eat for several days." Alberto said with concern. When he looked at Daniel, he easily saw the cute boyish look behind the sadness. Without hesitation, he stepped forward and gave Daniel a hug. This completely surprised Daniel. He could not believe that there were still some kind people in the world.

After a very light dinner, Daniel took the pills again and sat on the couch to watch the news with Alberto. The television was a small black and white set with rabbit ears and sat atop an antique mahogany round table with four curved legs.

"Daniel. To be honest, I could not keep you here or support you too long. I don't have too much money. After you have completely recovered, you will have to find another place for yourself." Alberto said with a sorry look on his face.

"I understand. Alberto. I am so appreciative of the help you have given me. Without it, I cannot imagine what would have happened to me." Daniel looked directly into Alberto's eyes intently.

Two days later, Daniel had almost completely recovered. He knew that he should not stay too long. He also didn't know how to thank Alberto for all of his help and kindness. He decided to tell Alberto that he would leave the next morning when he came back that evening. After dinner, Daniel said,

"Alberto, I will leave tomorrow. I don't know how to thank you enough." Daniel stepped forward and hugged Alberto emotionally. Alberto gently moved his face against Daniel's. Although this initially surprised Daniel, he responded in kind. Alberto slowly moved his lips to Daniel's and kissed him. From his previous experiences, Daniel now knew that Alberto must be homosexual.

To show his appreciation, Daniel kissed Alberto back passionately. Alberto took him to his bedroom. The bedroom was small with a full-size bed against the north side of the room. The lampshade was simple and gave the room a peaceful feeling because of its warm light. The window was slightly ajar, and a cool breeze blew through it. Alberto held Daniel in his gaze as he slowly undressed him. After taking off his own clothes, they embraced together on the bed with compassion. During sex with each other, Alberto turned Daniel onto his stomach and slowly penetrated him. It was uncomfortable at first, but Alberto was not forceful and took his time. This was Daniel's first experience of being penetrated and although it was a strange experience for him, the gratitude he felt for Alberto's help eased this and allowed him to open himself fully to the experience. Alberto asked Daniel to penetrate him as well. Eventually, together they orgasmed. It was a mutually enjoyable expression of appreciation and caring for both of them. They fell asleep in each other's arms.

The next morning after breakfast, Alberto said, "I know a place where you might have a chance to stay. I don't know how you might feel about it."

"I think any place is better than the street, Alberto. Don't you think so?" Daniel replied.

"I know a gangster group, or you may call it the local mafia, in Naples. I knew them for a couple of years because I contacted them a few times for sex partners. I know that if you cooperate and obey them, you will be taken care of nicely." Alberto said.

Suddenly, Daniel realized what place Alberto meant. It would mean joining the local gangster group that Daniel had always wanted to avoid and run away from. He began to hesitate. He kept silent for a moment thinking about what options he had. Live in the street or join the group. Without an ID card, he would always be just a refugee.

"Another choice is to go home." Alberto said.

Daniel was shocked to hear what Alberto said. Home sweet home was always on his mind for the last two and a half years. His eyes turned red with tears and sadness. After a while, he looked at Alberto and said,

"I will not and cannot go home like this. I am searching for the sun and I must find it. Furthermore, I don't have enough money to go home."

Those words implied Daniel's thought was of joining the gangster group. He had never tried, and he had always dodged them out of fear. He thought this option might be a chance to avoid hunger, living in the street, or getting sick without a place to go in the future. Finally, he nodded his head that he would join.

"This group is called New Heaven. The second leader, Rattlesnake, had a special relationship with me. I will contact Rattlesnake this morning to see what he says. You just stay here till tonight and I will let you know the result." Alberto said.

Daniel appreciated what Alberto tried to arrange for him, but he was not sure what path he would take for his future. Though he was still hesitant, he decided to try this new option; especially after his recent sickness. He realized that he could be very vulnerable when a major problem occurred. However, he still had to wait for the answer from Rattlesnake. He might be rejected and if he is, what would he do then? He pondered these things deeply after Alberto went to work in the morning.

When Alberto returned at 8 PM, Daniel was semi-anxious waiting for his answer. When Alberto entered the living room, he said,

"Rattlesnake will come to see you and maybe pick you up tonight. He said he had to meet you first before making a decision. He will be here around 9 o'clock. Here is some food I brought back. Let's eat something. Oh, yes, you should clean your body; especially your face. You have a cute boyish face." Alberto said. He knew this meeting would decide Daniel's future.

Daniel felt somewhat anxious, relieved, and hesitant. But he said: "Thank you, Alberto." He knew Alberto just wanted to help him, at least for the problem he had at the time.

They entered the kitchen and ate quickly. Afterwards, Daniel took a quick shower, shaved, and trimmed his hair. To any predator, he now looked handsome, juicy, and enticing. After all, he was only 19 years old.

About 9:05 PM, the doorbell rang, and Alberto went to the door to open it. He and Daniel were expecting Rattlesnake's visit.

"Hi, Rattlesnake. It's been a long time without seeing you. How are you?" Alberto gave him a hug like a very good friend. Rattlesnake greeted back and hugged Alberto as well.

When Rattlesnake saw Daniel next to Alberto, he knew that this must be the Daniel Alberto mentioned on the phone.

"This is Daniel. Daniel, this is Rattlesnake. Though his real name is Antonio. But he likes to be called Rattlesnake." Alberto introduced them.

Rattlesnake examined Daniel closely. A young, pure and naive heart could be very attractive to both male and female sexual predators. It would potentially bring good income to the family. He kept looking at Daniel with a smile just like a master in ancient Rome might inspect a slave to judge his value. Finally, Rattlesnake said,

"I think Big Head will like him."

They entered the living room and Alberto brought in some beer from the kitchen. Rattlesnake and Alberto were conversing in Italian and though Daniel's Italian was still poor, he could figure out what they were talking about. When they finished talking and drinking the beer, Rattlesnake informed Daniel that he had made a decision to accept him into New Heaven. He said to Daniel, "When we leave now, I am taking you to New Heaven's apartment where you will meet the others and begin your new life with the organization." Alberto and Daniel hugged one another, and Daniel felt so grateful for his friendship.

Even though Alberto had earlier explained to him what the organization was, Daniel was still not quite clear. Now, he knew that the organization or the family was called New Heaven. The leader was Big Head, Giovanni, about 37 years old. Rattlesnake was his right-hand man, the second leader of the family. Rattlesnake was only 29 years old. He was called this nickname because he was always complaining and making noise.

Except for Big Head, the entire New Heaven family shared an apartment in Naples. Big Head had his own apartment with his girlfriend a couple of blocks from New Heaven. In this family apartment, Rattlesnake had his own room on the second floor while all other 9 members, now 10 including Daniel, slept on the first floor. At the end of the second-floor corridor was an empty room for special guests.

Daniel and Rattlesnake arrived at New Heaven shortly after leaving Alberto's apartment. Rattlesnake assigned him a corner space with a clean mat, pillow, and blanket to sleep. Though it was not a comfortable bed, it was much more comfortable than being in the street. He also received some used and clean clothes to replace his old clothes he had worn for the past three years. He had not met Big Head yet. It seemed Rattlesnake had the authority to make decisions.

They had a floor heater in the apartment for winter's cold temperatures and there was always food in the kitchen for them to eat. There were two bathrooms for showering. In only a couple of days, Daniel knew all of the other 9 members who were all males ages from 14 to 25. It felt like a family, but it was strange that it seemed every family member kept some distance from each other. It had the feeling of family, but also that of an army unit.

Next morning, Rattlesnake asked one of the members called Paulo,

"Paulo, take Daniel to work today. He needs to know how to wash the cars, and sell drugs and flowers." Rattlesnake said.

Daniel knew that he must obey and follow Paulo. He needed to learn how to bring income to the family, otherwise, he would be punished or kicked out. In a couple of weeks, he had already learned how to earn money from various tasks and assignments. Selling drugs was the biggest profit, but illegal and dangerous. He knew that, but it was a job to bring income to the family. Rattlesnake would collect all the income earned each day from everyone during dinnertime. Without permission from Big Head or Rattlesnake, no body dared to keep any for himself.

* * *

Three weeks passed very quickly. During these three weeks, he saw Big Head three times. He came occasionally to have dinner with the family and listened to Rattlesnake's report. Now, Christmas was near. They all found a Christmas tree and decorated it. He felt like he was home since he had not celebrated with his family for almost three years.

It was a cheerful Christmas, and everyone received allowances and a gift from the New Heaven organization. Dinner was great, and everyone seemed joyful, but deep inside each one was a hidden sadness. They were all runaway kids from their homes. They truly missed the real families they had.

Three days later, an hour after they finished dinner, he was called to Rattlesnake's room. He knew Rattlesnake had always taken special care of him. He didn't know exactly why, but he knew Rattlesnake liked him since he had joined the group. He was curious as to why he was called by Rattlesnake tonight. All other members were either falling sleep or watching TV.

When he entered the room on the second floor, Rattlesnake was sitting on his bed with his underwear,

"Lock the door." He said.

Daniel locked the door behind and was wondering what the secret was. Why did Rattlesnake want the door locked?

"Come here! Close to me." Rattlesnake said.

He stepped forward curiously.

"Don't move!" Rattlesnake ordered and began to remove his own clothes. He was shocked and at the same time didn't know what to do. He was frozen there. Rattlesnake then pulled his pants and underpants down,

"Take all your clothes off." Rattlesnake ordered and waited for Daniel to finish doing what he had commanded.

Daniel's face turned flushed and he obeyed the order. He knew that if he didn't obey the order, the consequences could be serious. He took his pants, shoes, and socks off completely. He was completely naked. Now, he knew what Rattlesnake wanted to do to him. He also realized that's why he was treated especially well by Rattlesnake since he had joined New Heaven.

Rattlesnake began to kiss his body and gradually pulled him to the bed and made him lie on his back. He continued to kiss him and bite him. Though he felt some pleasurable stimulation, he also felt very uneasy and uncomfortable. After 20 minutes, Rattlesnake turned him over, tied his wrists and ankles to the bedposts, and finally raped Daniel. There was no compassion or tenderness; just violent lust and control. This was the first time Daniel was raped by a man and could not do anything to protect himself. He was immensely sad and felt powerless and hopeless. Compared with more than two years of suffering in different countries, joining New Heaven was really heaven since he had a warm place to sleep and plenty of food to eat. However, he had also lost his freedom and control of his body.

After that night, Daniel was called to Rattlesnake's room once a week and raped. It was not until nearly two months later that

Rattlesnake finally began to ignore him. It seemed Rattlesnake had gotten tired of him. However, Daniel also had a new job earning money for the family--sexual prostitution. He was rented out for sex both to male and female customers.

Now, almost once or twice a month, he was ordered to sleep with some rich and lonely women. Occasionally, he was ordered to have sex with men as well. Whenever he finished his services, he always received more reward than usual. He began to save some money since he did not have to worry about food. He wrote home and included a bank draft with it. Though there was not much, it would tremendously help his family financially. He received some letters from his parents who expressed their love and appreciation for his support. At least, he knew now that his family would not worry too much about him though they did not know what kind of job he had.

* * *

"Daniel, there is a job for you tonight. She is a regular customer of ours in these last two years. She is beautiful and sexy. She has not contacted us for a couple months. You are new and will be the best candidate we have for her. Here is her hotel address and be there at 8 PM tonight. By the way, her name is Rosanna." Rattlesnake handed him a piece of paper with the hotel address.

It was common that many customers who asked for sex used hotels instead of their residence. This was for their protection and also to avoid controversy from neighbors. Furthermore, they usually didn't want to build a long-term relation with any person they had sex with.

Daniel looked at Rattlesnake and simply nodded his head. He knew he did not have a choice. Obedience was the only way to survive in this New Heaven family. In addition, after a few times of sexual activities with different persons, he felt more or less like a sex machine. He knew that sex without love and compassion was just business. He didn't enjoy it.

He trimmed his hair short and shaved again. He tried to make himself as attractive and appealing as possible. He knew that was what customers wanted. He knocked the door of Rossana's hotel room at 7:58 PM.

"Please come in, the door is opened." A voice came from inside.

Daniel stepped in and saw a lady with a beautiful nightgown on sitting on a sofa. This was a very nice suite with a living room, bedroom, kitchen, and bathroom. "It must be expensive to rent it." Daniel thought.

"Good evening, madam. I am here for your service." Daniel said and bowed politely as a schoolboy or an obedient slave waiting to serve.

"My name is Rosanna. What is your name?"

"Daniel, madam." Daniel smiled and looked at her closely. "Yes, she is about 40 years old and beautiful." He thought.

"Just call me Rosanna." She stood up and took a detailed look of Daniel.

"You are new in New Heaven. I have not met you before." She looked at Daniel with greedy eyes.

"Turn around, Daniel." She ordered, and Daniel did.

"Not bad, not bad. No bad at all, young man." Rosanna said.

"Go to take a shower and wash yourself very clean. There is a man's nightgown in the bathroom." She continued.

"Yes, Rosanna." He went to bathroom and took a shower. He knew even though he had taken a shower before he came, customers usually demanded he have a shower or bath again. It seemed that they wanted to be sure that the meat was clean.

When Daniel came out of the bathroom and went to the sofa area,

"Drop your nightgown, Daniel." She ordered, and Daniel did. She walked around Daniel and took a detailed look again and this time, Daniel was naked completely. Though Daniel still felt somewhat uneasy, he was more used to it now.

Rosanna stepped forward, pulled Daniel's head forward, and kissed him savoring the first taste of her prayers. Daniel stood there without too much of a response but feeling some arousal. After a few seconds, he began to respond and cooperate. This made Rosanna excited. She began to play and bite his tongue. "Definitely, she is an expert." Daniel thought. Daniel began to learn how to dance with a partner and coordinate with her.

After a few minutes, Rosanna took Daniel's hand and entered the bedroom. Once they entered the room, Rosanna ordered Daniel lie down on bed facing down. She took some ropes from drawer and began to tie Daniel's four limbs on the corners of the bed. Daniel did not know what she would do to him, but he had a feeling that it would be a tough night.

After Daniel was tied up completely, she began to kiss and bite him gently. It brought Daniel to a greater level of arousal. Next, she used a short whip to whip Daniel. Daniel did not know how to respond when she began. Later, he realized that Rosanna was looking for Daniel's response and began to pretend he was in pain,

"Nnnnm! Ao!" Daniel began to groan. This had made Rosanna very aroused and happy.

After that, Rosanna untied him and had a sex with him in various positions. She was the teacher and he was the neophyte. She taught him well and he satisfied her hunger. It was an adventure and exciting for both of them. This was an experience that Daniel had never had. After sex, both of them were tired and fell asleep.

Rosanna gave Daniel $350,000 lire (US$200) the next morning after breakfast.

"I may ask for you again, Daniel. You look so pure, innocent, and obedient. That's the way I like it." Rosanna said.

"Yes, madam. I am glad that you enjoyed it." Daniel replied.

Though Daniel enjoyed it on some level, after all, they were not lovers. It was just business and a show. Rosanna was beautiful, but not the type of woman or person he liked. Again, he felt that he was just like merchandise or a sex machine. By now, he realized that if he did what the customer wanted, he could receive a bigger reward.

* * *

One day, about 10 months after he had joined New Heaven, one of his gang members brought back a 16-year-old boy who had run away from Czechoslovakia about six months before. This boy's name was Adam and he was hungry and looked very sloppy. He was so skinny that just by looking at him, you would feel sorry for him. All the New Heaven members greeted him. In a week or so, he was trained to beg since he was young and had a cute face that could earn sympathy easily. He also got along with everyone easily since he was simple and pure.

One Friday, Big Head was there for dinner and to listen to the report from Rattlesnake. This day, Adam also earned more money than he expected, nearly 185,000 lire, equivalent to US$110. He was so happy that he took some money and bought a pair of shoes without it being approved by Big Head or Rattlesnake. During the dinner, Rattlesnake discovered that he had a new pair of shoes.

"Where did these new shoes come from? Did you steal them?"

"No! Sir! I bought them with my own money."

"What do you mean your own money? Isn't it the money you earned today?"

"Yes! Since I had earned extra today, I decided to buy a pair of shoes for myself."

"Don't you know the rules here? You are stealing the family's money. All of the money you earned belongs to the family. Without approval, you cannot use it."

"It's not fair. I earned all of this." He began to argue. Immediately, he was pulled away from the dining table. Rattlesnake took him to an isolated room near the back of the apartment. Big Head was watching the development sitting at the dining table quietly with a solemn face.

Several minutes later, a very disturbing noise came out of the room. It was a mixture of beating, torture, crying, and begging for forgiveness. All of the family members were quiet and paid attention to what was happening in that room. About half an hour later, Rattlesnake came out of the room and entered the dining room,

"This is just to give you guys an example. Don't betray the family." He looked at everyone with serious and sharp eyes. He then left with Big Head who had not said one word throughout all of this.

Later, when Adam came out of the room, nobody dared to go to help him and show mercy. They all knew that it could be anyone of them in the future that would suffer a cruel punishment. Barely able to walk and in obvious pain, Adam crawled to his sleeping area and lay down without dinner. There was blood at the rear of his pants and his face was swollen and red with blood trickling down his chin. He was still crying.

Early in the morning at about 2 o'clock, one of the members, Romeo, woke up and went to the restroom. He nearly slipped and fell as he walked in there in the dark. When he turned on the light, he discovered that his feet were covered in blood. In shock, he quickly woke everyone up. After they turned on the light, they discovered that Adam had cut his own artery on his wrist. He had been dead for at least half an hour. Immediately, Romeo ran up to the second floor and woke up Rattlesnake to report the incident. Rattlesnake immediately called Big Head for further instructions. This was a big event and he could not make this decision by himself. After he received Big Head's directive, Rattlesnake asked two of the senior members to help him remove Adam's body outside. Obviously, they didn't report this to the police. They couldn't since the family was conducting illegal businesses. Although New Heaven had policemen that they paid to look the other way when it came to prostitution, this was different. It was a suicide resulting from severe physical abuse and torture.

About 2 hours later, they came back. The floor had been washed cleaned by another two members. Everyone was quiet, and nobody dared to speak about anything. A few days later, everyone in the family knew that Rattlesnake had placed the body on a bench in a public park about 10 miles away. When policemen discovered the dead body, they didn't know where he came from or who he was. All they knew was that he was another 'sun chaser' from an Eastern European country.

Seemingly without much choice, Daniel continued to live under these cruel, merciless, and practical conditions for another 13 months. He felt that he was a robot or a machine, numb without much feeling. He knew he had changed, changed to a different person who could not afford to have emotions in order to survive the harsh realities of gang life in Milan. It was now almost two years that he had been in New Heaven. He was 21 years old. He was still lost.

One night, he was awakened by a vivid nightmare and couldn't fall asleep again. Sweating and anxious, he sat up in his little corner of the apartment thinking and trying to sort out his future. He sighed, cried and felt such pity for himself. He was waiting, waiting for a chance...

* * *

One Sunday afternoon, when the group returned to the apartment for dinner, Daniel saw a gangster member named Santo bring three guests into the living room. New Heaven's leader, Big Head Giovanni, and Rattlesnake immediately stood up and welcomed these guests. This must be a special day since Big Head Giovanni had been waiting in the apartment since 5 PM and a feast was waiting to be served.

"Hi! Brother! It is great to see you again." Big Head Giovanni said and showed his Naples hand gangster greeting sign. Only allied gangster groups in different areas of Naples were able to recognize these gang signs.

"Hi! Brother! Me too! Me too!" The most senior guest replied and reciprocated with his gang sign as well. Then, he stepped forward to hug Big Head Giovanni and then Rattlesnake.

"It's been two years, Primo. Who are these two new guys with you?" Giovanni asked.

"This is Dante, and this is Nino." He introduced them to Giovanni.

When Daniel took a look at them, he guessed that the most senior one, Primo, was probably around his early 40's while the other two were only in their early 30's. Giovanni took them around and introduced them to the entire group of 12 people, including Big Head himself. From the other members, Daniel knew that these three guys belonged to a big gangster group in Milan. There were about 13 groups occupying the territory of Milan. The group led by Primo was the largest. They had 36 members. During the introduction, Daniel could feel that all three of them were like an eagle or lion hungry and searching for prey. Their sharp eyes scanned over every member; especially young ones.

Giovanni invited them to sit down with him at his table for dinner. About 30 minutes later, a chef brought out some spaghetti pasta, some meat, red wine, and salad. This chef was hired for this special occasion. That evening's dinner was better than usual. During the meal, while the three visitors were talking to Big Head and Rattlesnake, they also kept turning their heads toward Daniel and looking at him. Daniel could sense that they were talking about him. This gave him an uneasy feeling. A cold chill emerged from deep inside his bones. He didn't know what they were talking about. "Do they want to take me to Milan and join their group? Maybe I remind them of someone they knew." He thought.

After dinner, every New Heaven member stepped forward to hand in the money they had earned hustling that day. Each one received from 80,000 lire to 150,000 lire that was equivalent to US$50 to US$80. Daniel also stepped forward and handed in the money he earned from begging and washing car windows on the street. He received 95,000 lire. It was not the best day since it was Sunday. Usually, they earned much more money during weekdays.

When Daniel stepped forward, Rattlesnake took the money and recorded it in his handbook. As he walked away, he said,

"Wait a minute. Daniel." Daniel stood there perfectly still with his head down looking at the carpeted floor. His heart was beating very fast. He was very nervous.

"Are you sure he is the one you like?" Big Head asked Primo. Primo replied to him with a head nod.

"Daniel, come to my place at 7 o'clock tonight. Remember, punctually." Big Head said.

"Yes! Sir." Daniel replied with a trembling voice. He had always been afraid of Big Head and Rattlesnake since he saw the punishment little Adam received, the poor 16-year-old boy from Czechoslovakia. He knew that 'obedience' was always the main key to surviving in this gangster society. Deep in his guts, he was expecting a tough night.

* * *

He came to Big Head's apartment 2 minutes before 7:00 PM. He rang the doorbell and the voice through the telecom said "come in." The apartment building door was opened via remote control. Big Head was expecting his arrival. His apartment was only two blocks away from where the group stayed. Daniel had been here once before to deliver a letter to. He knew that Giovanni's apartment was on the second floor. He knocked on the door and Giovanni opened the door.

"Hi, Daniel! You know that we have three important allied guests from Milan today. They like you very much and wish you could offer them some entertainment and service tonight. Don't screw up! Otherwise, ...!" Big Head looked at him with sharp eyes.

Daniel knew that this was a serious warning. Big Head always showed this facial expression whenever he gave them a warning. Big Head used his left index finger to point to the last door on the right in the hallway.

"You'll be alone with them there tonight." He said and put his hat and jacket on. He left the apartment.

Daniel walked to the door. He took a deep breath and knocked. Nino, the youngest one among the three, opened the door.

"Come in!" A voice from inside commanded.

When he went in the room, he saw a chair was placed in the center of the room.

"Sit down!" Primo said dispassionately.

Then, they all looked at Daniel with a delightful smile. It seemed these hungry predators had found their prey and were waiting to slaughter it.

"What do you think? I believe that we have chosen the best one." Dante said with a smile.

"We haven't had this kind of meat for a long time." Nino looked at Dante laughing.

They were staring at him as if they were going to eat and swallow him alive. Daniel felt extremely uneasy and the chill feeling again emerged from deep inside his bones.

"Take your clothes off, slowly." Dante said.

He hesitated for a moment, then began to unbutton his shirt and then took off his T-shirt. His nice, toned, muscular body that he had developed during the past eighteen months was now on display.

"He looks tasty. Don't you think so?" Nino turned his head to Dante and said.

Daniel kept his head down to avoid eye contact with any of them. All he wished for this night was their mercy.

"Now! Take off your pants. Remember! Slowly. Ya! Also, your shoes and socks." Dante ordered.

He took his shoes and socks off. He stood up and unbuckled his pants. Now his muscular and good-looking thighs and legs could be seen. Daniel could sense their primal hunger and that, to them, he was but a piece of raw, delicious meat they could barely wait to devour.

"Take that off, too!" Finally, Primo said something. Until that moment, he had been very quiet and enjoyed the show.

Again, Daniel hesitated only momentarily and quickly took his underpants off. He knew clearly that if he obeyed every wish they had, he just might be treated nicer and mercifully.

Nino stepped forward and took the chair away.

"Turn around." He said. So, Daniel did.

"Not bad, no bad at all." Nino nodded his head.

They took him to the bathroom. They took their clothes off.

"Get inside the bath tub." Dante said. Daniel stepped in the tub. Dante stepped in also, turned the shower on, and began to wash Daniel's head and body. After 5 minutes, Nino also stepped in and again washed Daniel's body. It seemed they were washing their prey to keep it clean before slaughtering. After both of them washed Daniel, they also washed themselves clean. They stepped out.

"Stay here." Dante said.

Now, Primo stepped in. He was only watching when Dante and Nino were washing Daniel.

"Both of you wait outside." Primo said. Both Dante and Nino left the bathroom naked.

"Wash my body. Everywhere." He gave Daniel an order.

Daniel picked up the soap and began to wash Primo's body. After 7 minutes or so, Daniel finished his job. Primo brusquely pulled him closer, roughly kissed and hugged him. They showered for another 5 minutes and then came out.

"Lie down on the bed. Face up." Primo told Daniel.

As soon as Daniel was on the bed, Dante and Nino used rope to tie his arms and legs to the four legs of the bed. They covered his eyes and put a piece of tape over his month. He was absolutely helpless now. Terrified, he imagined this must be how a lamb waiting to be slaughtered felt.

Daniel was not sure who was doing what. All he could feel was this frenzy of them taking turns kissing, biting, spanking, and even whipping him. At the beginning, he kept quiet and as calm as possible. However, he soon realized that what they were looking for was a reaction from him from their prodding. Like cruel children pestering a trapped animal, they derived pleasure from its fear and pain. Daniel began making exaggerated noises of excitement and groaned with false pain. To his relief, he found they would not torture him further or as severely as long as he showed some excitement. After nearly 40 minutes of this game, they untied him, turned him over, bound his arms and legs and repeated the same thing. Finally, they raped him one after the other. By this point, Daniel had become numb and although he experienced pain from their violent penetrations, he had shifted his mind to thoughts of being in the sun living the life he so desperately dreamed of.

When they finally satisfied their carnal desires, they untied him.

"Get up! Dress up! You can go now." Primo said. It seemed that they were very satisfied with what they had asked Giovanni for. These men who went home to their wives, girlfriends and children did not consider themselves homosexual. It was about the need to exercise power over another human being to fill the vacuum of their hollow existence by preying on the helpless.

As he dressed himself, Daniel discovered his body was covered with bruises and teeth marks. He was so happy that the whole thing was over that he did not really care about his injuries. After he dressed up, Primo stepped forward and gave him some money,

"This is for you. You don't have to give it to Rattlesnake." He said.

Daniel took the money and left Giovanni's apartment. When he stepped out, he took a look at the money he received. He was surprised to see there were about 600,000 lire. It was equivalent to almost US$350. This confirmed for him that they had had a very good time at his expense, of course. When he returned to New Heaven, he lay down on his bed in the corner. What happened to him earlier just wouldn't leave his mind. He had been hurt so profoundly, and more psychically than just his body. He kept thinking about it over and over asking himself, "Is this the life I want?" "What future do I have?" "How will I ever find the sun remaining in this situation?" He knew that he was only a sexual slave and a money-making tool to satisfy his masters. The tears of despair bled uncontrollably from Daniel's eyes. As he felt some pain again from the bruises, he thought, "I must leave here and go far, far away!" He recognized that he would be alone living on the streets and possibly starving once he left the gangster family, but he would rather face that challenge than continue under the false support and safety of New Heaven. His heart and spirit were bursting for freedom and self-respect and he reminded himself aloud, "I must keep searching for my sun!!" With the money he had been saving over the past months, Daniel now had nearly US$600. This fueled his confidence that he would be able to successfully run away from New Heaven. Once he began thinking of a plan, he felt better and soon fell asleep.

* * *

On Monday, November 21, 1994, while Daniel was hustling in the streets, he noticed there were a few trucks parked near his territory. He walked over and talked to some of the truck drivers. He found out there was a truck leaving at 5 PM to Paris. He found the driver and talked with him.

"Hi! Sir! My name is Daniel and I wonder if you would kindly give me a ride to Paris. I was told your truck is going to Paris this afternoon."

The truck driver looked at him doubtfully.

"I don't have space for you. Furthermore, it would take about 2 days of driving to get to Paris."

Daniel could sense that this guy just didn't want any trouble; especially with a stranger for two days. This is why he rejected Daniels' proposal. Daniel took his money out and said,

"I can pay you 400,000 lire."

Now, the truck driver realized that Daniel was not asking for a free ride. He looked at the money and said,

"Give me 200,000 lire now and pay me the rest when you come this afternoon at 5:00 PM and you have a deal."

He was so happy to see that the truck driver changed his mind. He gave him 200,000 lire.

"I will see you at 5:00 this afternoon." Daniel said.

Daniel continued his street hustle for New Heaven washing car windshields to earn some money. At noontime, he went back to the apartment. He saw there were only a couple members there taking a nap. He took his backpack quietly and snuck out.

He came to the truck parking area 10 minutes before 5:00 PM and found the truck driver. He was getting ready to take off.

"Get in! We are leaving now. You will be in the back seat. You may put your backpack there."

He turned his head to a place about 20 yards away where there was a guy about 35 years old talking to another truck driver. He shouted,

"Uberto! We are leaving."

Uberto ran quickly to where Daniel was.

"This young guy will go with us to Paris." He said.

"What's your name, young man?" Uberto asked as he jumped in the truck with Daniel.

"Daniel, sir!"

"Don't call me sir! Just Uberto."

The driver also finally introduced himself. His name was Zanipolo. This exchange of names somehow made Daniel feel warm and safe.

As the truck left the area, Daniel finally felt free. He knew no one would search for him until nearly 8 o'clock that night, the time for handing in the day's income and to eat dinner. It was only 5 o'clock which was the busiest traffic time and for money making. He calculated that in just two hours he would probably be in Rome. As he thought of this, he smiled spontaneously. When they took off, Daniel gave Zanipolo the balance of money as promised.

France

Two days later, the truck arrived in Paris at nearly midnight. The weather had already turned cold in Paris this time of the year; especially since it was a rainy day when they arrived. After two days together, Daniel had built a good relationship with them; especially Uberto.

"Do you have a place to stay tonight Daniel?" Zanipolo asked.

"No! Sir." Daniel replied. He did not know what to do or if he could do anything. After he paid Zanipolo, he didn't have much money left and he needed to save money as much as possible for any unknown concerns in Paris. Hotels were just too expensive for him.

"Come stay with me tonight. A couple of friends and I rent a small apartment here." Uberto said. Zanipolo always slept in a hotel. They would stay only a day or, at most, two, then they would return to Italy for another shipment.

"That will be great. Uberto." Daniel looked at him with sincere appreciation.

"However, you cannot stay longer than tonight. You know, I have two roommates. We shared the rent together. The apartment is very small. In addition, I will leave Paris again with Zanipolo in a day or two."

"I understand, Uberto. Even just the one night, has already helped me a lot."

Uberto took him to a suburb of Paris, Saint-Ouen, by subway. It was late. They were lucky because there were only one or two more trains scheduled, then no more. When they arrived at the metro station, they walked about 15 minutes and came to an old building. Uberto entered the building and led Daniel to the third floor. When Uberto opened the door with his key, they saw two roommates sleeping on the floor. The apartment was very small as Uberto had said. They didn't make any noise and just found a spot to lie down quietly. They fell asleep very quickly since both of them were very fatigued.

When Daniel woke up, he realized that two roommates were already gone working and Uberto was in the tiny kitchen cooking some food and making coffee. It was almost 9 o'clock in the morning. After sleeping so well, Daniel felt much better. He walked into the kitchen and said,

"Uberto! Thank you very much. You are a nice man."

"No problem! When I travel around, people always helped me too. Come, let's have some food and coffee."

Daniel sat down and Uberto brought some food to the small apron-covered table. When they began to eat, the telephone rang, and Uberto went into the other room and picked up the phone,

"Halloo! This is Uberto." He answered. He talked a couple of minutes on the phone. Even though Daniel was in the kitchen, he could hear some of the conversation. He heard Zanipolo on the other end of the phone line tell Uberto that they would take off and return to Naples tonight. Now, Daniel knew that after breakfast, he must leave. After Uberto finished his conversation on the phone, he came in the kitchen,

"It was Zanipolo. We will leave tonight. Back to Naples." He paused for a moment and continued,

"I am sorry that you cannot stay here tonight."

"I understand, Uberto! I have to find some job anyway. After breakfast, I must leave."

An hour later, Daniel left Uberto's apartment and took the train into Paris. He believed he might have a better chance to make it in central Paris instead of its suburbs.

This was Daniel's first time ever in Paris. He didn't know how French people would respond to him begging. He didn't know how much chance he actually had finding any job; especially because he did not speak French. Later, he realized that it was even harder than he imagined finding a job in Paris. The French government was very serious and forbade companies hiring anyone without a proper ID card.

Though Paris still had some tourists even in November, there were much fewer compared with summer. Daniel needed to dress neat and keep himself clean. This way, he might have at least a chance to elicit someone's generosity. One night, when it was colder than usual, the streets were almost empty. He was hungry and came to the night tourist area where many restaurants were. He could not help himself and knelt down at the corner of a store. He was hoping someone would pay attention to him.

After nearly one hour or so, it was nearly 10:30 PM. He was even more hungry and cold. He was so afraid that he might catch a cold and get sick again. A middle-aged lady just stepping out of a restaurant spotted him and paused a while looking at him. Daniel looked back at her smiling with an unspoken plea for help. The lady came to him,

"Would you like to make some money by staying with me tonight?" She asked.

Unfortunately, Daniel did not know what she said since he did not know French. This woman then tried speaking awkwardly in English and gestured with her hands to express her desire. Finally, Daniel figured out what she wanted. He nodded his head.

First, the lady bought some food for him from a convenience store nearby. She knew he must be hungry; particularly it being such a cold and late night. Then she took him back to her hotel a couple of blocks nearby.

Once they entered her room, she showed Daniel the bathroom and used her hand gestures again to ask Daniel to take a shower. Daniel complied if for no other reason that he would be able to get warm and clean in the shower. He had also learned that once you committed to be a customer's sexual object, it paid to conform to the wishes of the customer. He came out of the shower clean and ready to do what he was hired to do.

Though they couldn't communicate with each other easily, they clearly understood the language of sex. Daniel had learned many lessons from his previous encounters and was no longer an awkward lover. Although this woman was old enough to be his mother, he easily matched her experience sexually and pleased her immensely. Together, they enjoyed the evening and each other. From the last four years, Daniel had already learned that in order to be safe, a condom was required. He was delighted that most customers agreed with this and, usually, they would provide the condom. This woman did the same. He received 1200 francs (US$200) when he left her hotel. Now, he had enough money for a few days, but still unable to pay for lodging.

Daniel knew he could make more money easily selling sexual favors. However, as a Christian, he knew he shouldn't, and he always felt deeply guilty and sinful in his heart. He wished he had a better choice for surviving. He also clearly understood that he needed to be wary of local gangsters as well as the police although French policemen did not seem as preoccupied with vagrants as much as Italian's. To avoid unwanted gangsters' attention, Daniel moved from place to place often. For sex, he targeted single women and men rather than people in groups.

After servicing a couple more customers in two weeks, Daniel had earned additional money. However, because Paris was an expensive city to live in, he also spent more money as well. One day, when he was hanging around by the River Seine looking for opportunity, another refugee spotted him. However, this refugee was around 19 years old and wore very nice clothes.

"Hey! What is your name?" He walked toward Daniel speaking in Russian.

It was easy to recognize a refugee from the clothes and facial expression. This refugee spoke Russian since he knew that all the refugees were from eastern European countries and they somewhat spoke the same language. From his accent, Daniel could recognize that he was from Romania. He replied in Romanian.

"My name is Daniel Eraclid and I am from Romania. From your accent, I believe you are also from Romania." Daniel replied.

"Wow! That's great. My name is Marius, Marius Albert. I am from Craiova. Where are you from?" Marius asked.

"Turda. A small town near Cluj-Napoca." Surely, Daniel was so happy to meet another refugee from the same country. He knew Craiova, a bigger city on the south of Romania. However, he did not know too many Romanian who knew his town, Turda. He wondered and was curious how it could be Marius had such nice clothes and shoes.

They found a bench to sit down along the river to chat. Now, Daniel had a chance to take a good look at this young man. Marius was a little bit shorter than him, but looked younger, good looking, simple, pure, and naive.

"When did you leave Romania?" Marius asked.

"More than four years ago. When did you leave?" Daniel asked back.

"Two and half years ago." Marius replied.

"How do you survive in Paris? From your dress, it seems you are living pretty decent." Daniel wondered.

"Well. Actually, there is a local organization that takes care of refugees." Marius said.

This gave Daniel some hope that he might be able to survive and make it in Paris after all.

"I can ask my boss, Pascal, and see if he can accept you as well. We live outside of Paris and come into Paris every day for business." Marius continued.

"What business you are talking about?" Daniel asked.

With a little bit of hesitation, Marius replied,

"We sell drugs and sex. It is our major income for the organization."

This had proved Daniel's doubt about his nice dress. Now, he confirmed that Marius belonged to a local mafia. He regretted that he told Marius his real name. If the word ever got down to New Heaven, he would be in big trouble. To New Heaven, Daniel had betrayed them.

65

If they found and caught him, the consequence could be quite serious. When he thought of Big Head and Rattlesnake, chills racked his bones. He did not know if this organization had a connection with New Heaven. He kept quiet for a moment. He also knew that if he did not join this local mafia, they would hunt him down since he was their competitor. Without showing his fear,

"Please let me think of it for a couple days. I will see you here this Friday. OK?" Daniel asked.

"No problem. I believe Pascal will take you. You are a good looking guy and in the right age range for the family business." Marius replied.

He really regretted that he told Marius his real name. He was just careless and excited to meet another person like himself and momentarily let down his guard. He must learn not to trust other people easily. The more he thought about it, the more he felt scared. Now, he recognized that he might have less than one week to hide and run away from Paris.

From the last few sex jobs he did, Daniel still had about 800 francs in his pocket. The weather was getting cold again. He knew that it was better to go south. The weather would be warmer than Paris in winter. Without too much thought, he bought a train ticket Eurail France–Spain Rail Passes to Madrid. It cost him 650 francs and took nearly 10 hours of travel. On Friday, February 10, 1995, he arrived in Madrid. Daniel wondered what reaction Maruis would have when he could not find him at their agreed meeting point on the River Seine.

4
DESTINY

Mysterious Destiny

When Daniel arrived at the Madrid train station, he began to realize that he might be able to survive much easier in Spain than in Paris. The most important reason for this was he had stayed in Italy for more than 18 months and could more or less understand Spanish. Like Italian, Spanish was also derived from Latin and, therefore, similar. Because he had experienced frequent contact with his sex customers, Daniel was now able to speak Italian fluently.

He had only about 150 francs (US$25) in his pocket. He knew this would not last too long. He must find some way to earn money quickly. When he changed his French currency into Spanish Peseta, he received only 3000 Peseta. To get more money, he began begging in the train stations. Though he did receive some Pesetas here and there, this would not help much. Additionally, he had to pay attention to other beggars in the stations. He was aware that all of them belonged to local gangster organizations. If he were not cautious and was spotted, the consequence could be unimaginable. He could be beaten severely or even killed. If he was lucky, he might be convinced to join them. However, this was not what he wanted anymore.

Whenever he could, he also searched for food in garbage cans when there was no one around. Often, people threw away unfinished food in the garbage cans in the station. From his past experience, he spotted a couple pickpockets. He knew he must avoid encountering them. There was no doubt that they belonged to local gangsters. After he stayed near the station for a week or so, he realized that he might have been spotted. A local gangster might have caught his abnormal activities. He knew he must move on to other places. He knew that another place to try was Madrid's downtown area.

He took the bus there. It surprised him that he was able to find food and received help much easier from charitable people than in the train station. Except for a couple of times, he didn't see any possible gangsters around. He often went to the night streets where there were a lot of shops and restaurants. There were many street performers entertaining on the streets. He saw several who had good talent had earned handsome amounts of money. He thought of doing the same, but he didn't have any special talent to perform. Only after a few days, he realized that all of these street performers need licenses and that policemen checked them almost every couple of days. He also learned that these performers must pay taxes for their income. Now, he suddenly began to understand that this territory had been watched and controlled by the biggest legal mafia of all, the government. "This is the reason that not too many gangsters are here." He reasoned.

He realized that it was pretty safe when he begged for food or money. Usually, policemen would not pay attention to beggars. However, he also needed to be careful because he was an illegal foreigner. If he was ever caught, he might be jailed or deported out of the country. Many shops closed earlier. Usually, these shops would be opened until 1:00 AM; especially Friday and Sunday. The streets were usually crowded with people on these two days. One weekday night it was nearly 11 PM and almost all the streets were empty due to the windy, rainy weather. He saw some shops were closing. When he saw an old man and lady were closing their shop and were moving many items in front of the door, he came to help them. The lady was not quite happy about his help at the beginning, however, since the drizzling had turned into heavy rain and they could not move the goods into the shop in time, she didn't reject him. After half an hour of moving, all of the goods were inside without too much damage from the rain. The old man realized that if they didn't have this young dirty beggar's help, they might have lost a lot of money. At the end,

"Thank you! Young man." The old man said appreciatively, looked at him kindly, and handed Daniel 500 lire (US$25).

"You are welcome and thank you." He bowed to both of them with a smile.

Now, he realized that if he searched around, he might find many chances like this since there were so many shops. This could be a good way to earn money. He believed that if he could keep himself clean, he would not be perceived to be like a sloppy and dirty old man. He bought a pair of scissors, shaving cream, and also a shaving razor blade one more time. He had not cleaned his body for some time now. It was the second morning and the streets were still empty. He found a container in an alleyway and filled it with water from free spring water provided on the street. He came to a shop's big window and used it as a mirror to cut his hair short using the scissors. Then, he shaved his mustache and beard. When he looked at himself in the window, he couldn't believe that he was still young. He also took his shirt off and tried to clean his body. However, the weather was cold in the morning and the water was also cold. "How I miss the warm shower so much!" He felt. A nice, long hot shower would make him feel so rejuvenated right now.

He believed, that with his new look, he might have a better chance to find some work. However, after he had tried for many days, it didn't work as he expected. Most of workers in the shop were strong and didn't need his help. However, whenever he was running out of money, if he came to the shop owned by the old man and lady, often, he was called for help. He knew that they didn't need help sometimes. However, they still called him, so they could help him as well. Later, he realized that this old man and lady were a couple. His son was taking time off for vacation with his new wife. Therefore, they were taking care of the shop temporarily until his son's return. That meant he might just lose his opportunity to earn some money when their son returned in a couple more weeks.

It was the middle of October now, and the weather turned colder and bitter. There were fewer and fewer people on the street. That meant his chance of earning income from begging was less and less. Furthermore, the son of that old couple had returned and he seldom saw them in the shop again. Daniel saw their son and his new wife were there to handle the business. For Daniel, daily surviving had become very challenging. Especially now that those street performers were disappearing, he had to be even more careful since policemen had more time and the chance to catch him. He began to consume the money he had saved in the last six weeks. Again, he was thinking of going back to Romania. However, he wouldn't have enough money to travel. "What should I do?" "Should I join the local mafia again for surviving?" He thought. After a few minutes, he said to himself, "No! My dream is not been dead yet. I chased the sun but was lost. I must find it!" He tried to rebuild his confidence. However, it seemed harder with each year that had passed. "It had been 6 years already." He thought and felt depressed.

As was his routine, he cleaned his hair and face this morning. He came to the street to beg again. Though there were a few passersby that gave him some money, it was not enough. Additionally, he faced the nightly stress of finding some place to sleep now. He could not just sleep on the street like in the summer time. It was getting colder every night. This day, after sunset, he found a few pieces of bread and hamburger in the garbage can right in front of the McDonald's. After he ate, he came to a bench to sit there. "I must find a warm place for tonight. It seemed that it might rain tonight." He thought.

When he was sitting there, a middle age lady came forward and sat next to him.

"Hi! Young man! How are you doing?"

"I am fine! Thank you." He used some poor Spanish to answer this lady.

"It seemed that you are from another country."

"Yes, madam! I am from Romania."

"I heard that life is very difficult there now. You know, after the Communist party collapsed, the economy was pretty bad there."

"I don't know, madam! I left Romania 6 years ago and I don't have any news from there." Though his Spanish was not good, he could catch some idea of what the lady was talking about.

"Where do you live, young man?"

"On the street, madam!" He looked down embarrassed.

"Do you want to go home with me? You can sleep in my home tonight. I am alone."

"Thank you, madam! I am afraid that I will cause you too much trouble." From his experience, he knew that this was a hint that she needed his companionship tonight.

"Not at all. Come!" The lady stood up.

"Thank you very much, madam." He stood up.

He followed the lady to a three-story brick building that was 6 blocks from the night street. The lady used the key to open the main door and brought him up to the second floor where her apartment was. When they entered the room, the lady could see him much clearer. She smiled at him and said, "Treat yourself like you're at home. Nobody is here except you and me. Please sit on the couch."

However, Daniel felt that he was dirty and sloppy. He should not make the furniture dirty with his clothes. He kept standing in the living room. He took a look of the apartment; he knew this was an expensive apartment, elegant and luxury.

The lady went into her bedroom and came out with a set of clean towels and some male underwear.

"This underwear belonged to my old boyfriend. You can use it. They are useless now. Take a nice shower and make yourself clean. All of the shaving things are in the bathroom."

He bowed to the lady and took the underwear and towels from her hands. He knew that he must be very clean tonight. That's what all customers wanted.

This was the first time he had a nice warm bath since he left France 10 months earlier. He shaved again and used the scissors in the bathroom to trim his hair neat and short. He brushed his teeth and cleaned his body twice with soap. Then, he cut his finger and toe nails short and put some male perfume on his body. It took him nearly 40 minutes to finish the whole thing. He knew he must be clean, felt juicy, fresh, and yummy tonight. He was just like a nice attractive meal to the lady. This was also a good chance for him to earn some money as well.

After he cleaned up and put on the clean underwear, he came into the living room. When the lady looked at him, she was so happy to see that he was a handsome young man. She gave him a pair of pajamas and a pair of slippers. She had already warmed up some dinner and placed it on the dining table. There were also two candles lit on the table.

"Come here! Sit on this chair. Let's have something to eat. I am Mary. Just call me Mary, not madam anymore." The lady looked at him with a big smile. She poured some red wine for him.

"Thank you, madam! I am sorry. Mary. My name is Daniel." He sat down with a very polite manner.

"How old are you now?"

"I am 22 years old. I left home when I was 16."

"I hope you don't mind keeping an older lady company. You know! I just passed my 40th birthday."

"Of course not, Mary!" He hesitated a bit whenever he called her name.

Mary tried to ease his feelings of embarrassment. She knew that he was a nice young man. They ate dinner and drank. When they finished, it was nearly 8 PM.

"I need to take a bath. Do you mind helping me wash my back?"

"Naturally!" Daniel just tried to make Mary happy tonight.

They came into the bathroom and Daniel served her as she wished. After the bath, they went to bed together. Next morning at about 7:00 AM,

"Thank you, Daniel. I had a very good time last night. I need to go to work today. You must leave in 20 minutes. I am sorry." Mary said.

"I understand, Mary."

Mary went to her closet and picked up a few clothes and came out. She gave Daniel clothes and 40000 Peseta (US$200).

"Get rid of your old clothes. They don't look good."

"May I keep them still?" He asked.

"Of course."

Daniel went to the bathroom and picked up his dirty old clothes and put them into his backpack. Actually, what he wanted was a couple of t-shirts and underwear that had been with him since he left Romania. Whenever, he wore these, he felt warm. This underwear also would remind him of his original purpose, searching for the sun. When they came to the door of the apartment preparing to leave, Mary said,

"I may see you again next week. Don't come here. I will come to get you if I need you."

Except for his shoes, Daniel now had nice clothes to wear. To complete his wardrobe, he went to a shoe store and bought a cheap and comfortable pair. He knew that he had sufficient money to survive for at least a week comfortably. He continued to conserve his spending and hoped that he would have the chance again next week with Mary. Now, with his nicer clothes, he knew policemen wouldn't bother him. He went to a bookstore and purchased an Easy Learning Spanish booklet for tourists. He knew that in order to thrive here, he would need to better communicate with people in their language.

The next morning, the sun was good and warm. It was rare to see such a nice and warm weather in November. At the early morning, he took his dirty clothes out and washed them with soap. Then, he came to a park and placed his clothes on the benches. However, even though it was Friday, more people came in the park because of the nice weather. Though the clothes were not completely dried, he put them into the backpack to avoid attention. Fortunately, the weather was warm for about three days. Before it turned into rain and cold, he had already dried the clothes. He changed into his old clothes and threw away those that were really tattered. He put the good clothes he got from Mary in the backpack. These were now his working clothes which he needed to keep nice and clean.

Another week passed. With his nice outfit on that he received from Mary, Daniel waited for Mary's appearance. This Friday night, Mary again came. They had a very good time together again that evening. She paid Daniel another 40000 Peseta. He kept a good relationship with Mary for six weeks. They met once a week, always on Friday, except the first time, Thursday.

December came. The weather was much colder now. Though Daniel had warm clothes and some money, he couldn't afford to spend any for a hotel room. All the money he had would last only three nights if he rented one. Furthermore, he could not afford to pay rent for an apartment either. This Friday, again, he waited for Mary. Mary did not come this time and he didn't know why. "It seemed that we always had a good time and she enjoyed it very much." He wondered.

He was disappointed because he really needed the money to survive. He thought that there had to be some special reason Mary didn't come. "She will come next week." He hoped. However, Mary didn't come again the following week. He decided to visit her apartment area to see if he might catch her. After 6 weeks of good relations with her, he felt more comfortable going to her apartment rather than waiting for her to come to him as she had originally instructed him to do. However, when Daniel was within about a hundred yards away from her apartment building, he saw Mary leave the building with another man and enter a taxi together. Now, he understood that Mary might have a boyfriend. He realized that his role in her life was only temporary and it was business, not personal. It was crystal clear to Daniel that he must find a new way to make money. There were only a few people on the street this time in December. Begging would not be a good option. In the third week of December, his money ran low again. He began to eat only two meals a day. Most times it was only bread and some jam.

This Wednesday, December 13th, he again sat on the bench at about 5 PM in the afternoon. The sun would be gone in an hour or so. Temperatures dropped quickly. A gentleman with a windbreaker coat approached him.

"Hi! Do you want to make some cash?"

Daniel knew that this guy meant to sell his sex for money. He looked at the guy with a smile. He shook his head negatively and this gentleman started walking away. When Daniel thought about how he was going to live in the next few days, he realized he needed this job urgently. After a minute of hesitation, he ran after the gentleman and said,

"I am sorry, sir! I really need some money."

"You will be paid handsomely. What's your name?"

"Daniel, sir!"

"Come with me, Daniel, please."

They went to the main street. This guy called a taxi and told the driver to go to a nice hotel where he was staying. He and Daniel barely spoke. They went into the hotel room. Daniel knew this gentleman was a businessman from their initial conversation and how the man was dressed. He also knew that he was not local since he stayed at the hotel. Daniel also thought this gentleman might come from Germany since he had some German accent in his Spanish. When they entered the room, he decided to talk to him in German,

"May I ask where are you from? You seem to have a German accent."

This surprised the guy.

"Yes! I am from East Germany. I will be here for the next couple of days for business." This guy was happy to know that Daniel was able to speak German. He asked,

"Which country were you from? You are not Spanish either."

"I'm from Romania, sir."

"How old are you?"

"I am 22, sir!"

"You don't have to call me sir! Just Michael." He took a detailed look at Daniel. "Not a bad looking boy!" He thought. He then continued,

"Go to take a shower and clean yourself good."

Daniel went into the bathroom and took his clothes off. He heard the door's knocking. He opened it with a gap. Michael pushed it open and stepped in.

"Let's take a shower together."

This was a surprise. However, from his past experience, some of his customers liked to take a shower or bath with him. Michael took his clothes off and took a couple pieces of ropes from drawer. Daniel looked at his action and knew that he might have a tough night tonight.

"Put your hands behind you."

Daniel did. Michael tied his hands behind him and his legs too. He then filled the tub with half of the water. He used the soap to wash Daniel's body very thoroughly. Daniel felt very uncomfortable at first. However, after a few minutes, when he realized that Michael didn't actually want to harm him, he felt better. In a few minutes, he began to feel excited from the physical stimulation. Michael also took a shower. After the shower, Michael untied him. With reddened eyes, he had a mixture of sorrow and excitement. When they came out of the shower, Michael said,

"Daniel. I don't know if you experienced what I wish to do before or not. However, just obey my wishes tonight. I will pay you handsomely." He looked at Daniel with eagle eyes watching his prey.

This chilled Daniel to his core. He saw this same gaze before when he was sexually abused by those three men in Italy. However, he couldn't renege now. He desperately needed money. Once again, he felt like a lamb waiting to be slaughtered. He just wished Michael would show some mercy. He looked at Michael and nodded his head in agreement with his wishes.

"Lie down on the bed." Michael said. So, Daniel did.

Michael tied him up on the bed and used all kind of methods to satisfy his sexual desires. Fortunately, he didn't physically harm Daniel. "Compared with the other three men who had raped and abused him, he has some consideration for me." Daniel thought.

After nearly two hours, finally, Michael seemed satisfied.

"Thank you!" He said and while he was putting his clothes on, he told Daniel,

"You may leave now."

After Daniel got dressed, Michael gave him US$150. To east European people, this was a lot of money. However, compared with what other customers had paid him previously, this was not as much. He didn't know if he enjoyed the action even though he felt excited at times during the experience. He also knew that if he were not excited, usually, the customer would torture him more.

"I will be still here tomorrow. I like you. Do you want to make more money tomorrow night?" Michael asked.

Daniel looked at Michael and saw Michael seemed to be begging. Now, he didn't know who was the one in control? He knew that physically, Michael would be his master; however, mentally and emotionally, Daniel now felt perhaps that he was the one in charge of the situation.

"OK! I will meet you again tomorrow night."

"Be here at 8 PM. I will be here waiting for you."

Next morning, Daniel went to the bank to purchase a bank draft for US$100. It wasn't too much by Spanish standards; however, to him this was a lot of money. He mailed the check back to his Mom. "Papa and Mama will need this money for Christmas." He thought. This was the second time he had sent money home. He sent some money home about 16 months ago when he was in Italy. He also included a letter inside and told his parents that he was good and healthy. He had been working hard and wished that he could send more money for them. He just kept some for himself. He knew that he would have more tomorrow night. The second day, he went into a restaurant and ordered a meal. This was the first time that he went into a restaurant by himself for a nice and decent meal. He felt like a king even though he knew that it was only an illusion. However, he had to have a way to forget or numb his pain sometimes; especially this time of the year. Christmas was a torturous holiday for most street people he had known.

The next day, he came to see Michael again. Before arriving, he hid his backpack and money in a secret place. Though this evening, he was treated similarly to the previous night, Daniel was mentally prepared this time. He knew exactly how Michael liked his sexual pleasures. He would occasionally pretend that he was suffering from Michael's torturing while also enjoying its excitement. This made Michael very happy and he felt less guilty about his actions. Michael paid Daniel US$200 this time. Daniel believed this money would help him for a couple weeks.

"I must leave tomorrow. I would like to thank you. Daniel. I will miss you."

Since then, Daniel had never seen him again. When he came out of Michael's hotel around 11 PM, he realized that two guys were following him. He had never seen them before since he was always in the night street area. He knew that he might have intruded into some local gangster's territory. He tried to stay with the crowd. However, before he arrived at the train station, they caught up with him.

"Hi! Brother!" A guy said behind him.

He could sense that he was in danger. Without hesitation, he began to run. Unfortunately, he was caught after nearly 500 yards. He was tangled down onto the ground. They punched him and kicked his stomach. He saw this when he was in Germany when eight skinheads were beating up the Czechoslovakia boy, Henry. All he could do was to curl up his body into a ball and cover his head with both hands to protect himself. His nose was bleeding, and his stomach was in pain. He just hoped that he was not seriously injured. It would be an unimaginable disaster if he were injured since he couldn't afford to see a doctor. He just tightened his body as much as he could. After they had beaten him for five minutes, they searched his pocket and took all of his money.

"Keep away from this area. If we see you again, we'll beat you up again." One of them said.

He got up with pain. He didn't have any money in his pocket. It took him nearly two hours to walk back to the night street again. When he arrived, he went to his hiding place where he hid his backpack. "Fortunately, it is still here." Now, all he had was about 10000 (US$65) to survive. He sat down and couldn't help but to cry. "What should I do?" His good clothes were torn and dirty and his entire body was covered with bruises. However, he felt grateful since there were no bones broken. Now, in this miserable condition, he had to face the hardest time of the year. It would be Christmas soon. He had to conserve all of the money he had. Often, he came to some department stores and begged for money. Because it was Christmas time, he could still earn some money through begging. However, his actions also made the storeowners very unhappy since he might scare some customers away. They called the police at times and he had to be very careful not to be caught and arrested. Days passed very quickly, and his reserved money kept steadily diminishing.

It was now Christmas Eve, the dark Sunday. To all of the people who had family around them, tonight would be a joyful and happy night. However, to him, this was the darkest day of the year. He had always been so homesick at this time of the year in the last six years. When he thought of his Mom and family, his eyes turned red and filled with tears. He knew his parents would have worried about him very much. He was also wondering where his two good friends were who had also run to chase the sun.

After he ate a couple of pieces of bread, he came to the corner of a department store. He was still hungry. He knew that it would be a lot of leftovers thrown away in the garbage cans tomorrow. All of the shops were closed except a few bars, and there was no one on streets. He squatted down and curved his body near the entrance area of the department store since the weather was a mixture of sleet and snow. It was a cold and wet night. He was sitting there and thought about what he should do next. His body was shivering. "Should I join the local gangster group or not?" "They may not accept me and beat me up instead." He thought.

While he was thinking and feeling morose, he saw an old man with a clutch coming out of a bar just across the street of the department store. The old man walked haltingly. He was pretty drunk. He looked at the old man and was wondering why this old man was also alone tonight and drunk on Christmas Eve. "It's not only me who was unfortunate." He thought.

Suddenly, he saw the old man slip and fell to the ground. His clutch had been thrown a few yards away. Daniel quickly got up and ran to him. He saw his wallet was on the ground and some money was spread out on the wet ground. "The wallet must have come out of his jacket pocket when he fell." He thought. When Daniel looked closely, he saw many bills with 20000 pesetas were on the ground. To him, this was a lot of money. "There is no one around. I can take his wallet and money and run. Nobody will ever find out." His evil mind was thinking. However, there was another voice, "No! You can't. You just left the society of those that take what they don't earn and hurt others for no reason; you cannot step in again." His good mind argued. After a couple minutes of debating with himself, Daniel picked up the money and wallet. He stepped forward and tried to help the old man stand up.

Again, he was wondering why this wealthy old man was in the bar until almost midnight on Christmas Eve.

"Where is your home?" Daniel asked the gentleman. When he looked at the old man, he could see that he was about 65 years old. He helped the old man to stand up again. He handed him his wallet.

"This is yours, sir!"

The old man looked at him bleary-eyed. He used his finger to point to the direction of where his home was. Daniel then helped this old man to walk toward his home. After 15 minutes of walking, under the old man's guidance, they came to an apartment building located in the rich and luxury neighborhood. The old man took his key out and tried putting it into the keyhole but failed. He gave the key to Daniel,

"Open it for me, please, young man."

When Daniel opened the door, they entered a very fancy and luxuriously appointed apartment. He helped the old man take off his jacket and shoes and slowly walked with him to the living room. The old man sat down on his sofa and began to wake up. After a few minutes, he stood up by himself from the sofa and walked toward the kitchen to fix some tea. When Daniel saw this, he helped him to the kitchen. It seemed the old man could handle himself much better now. However, Daniel still followed him to the kitchen just to be sure. When he entered the kitchen, he saw a piece of leftover cake on the dining table. He kept looking at it and it caught the old man's attention.

"Are you hungry?" The old man asked.

Daniel nodded his head slightly smiling.

"Sit down." He said.

A few minutes later, the tea was ready. The old man poured a cup of tea for Daniel and a cup for himself.

"Eat the cake! You will feel better!" The old man got a fork from the kitchen drawer and gave it to him.

"Would you like some, sir?" Daniel asked.

The old man shook his head and sat down on the other side of table.

"Where is your home, Young man?"

"I have no home, sir! I live in the streets."

The old man looked at him and entered into a deep state of pondering while Daniel was eating the cake. "What a delicious chocolate cake!" He thought. He had never had such a good tasting cake in his whole life. When he finished, the old man looked at him and smiled,

"Would you like to stay here tonight? It's cold outside." The old man kindly asked.

"But it will bring you too much of trouble."

"Don't worry about it. Come with me."

He took him upstairs to a bedroom and took some towels out of the closet. He gave them to Daniel.

"The bathroom is two doors down the hallway. Take a shower and sleep. I am tired, and I want to go to sleep now. Take care of yourself." The old man said and went to the end of the hallway. He entered his bedroom.

Daniel had never been treated so nicely and kindly since he ran away from home. He took the towels and went into the bathroom. Everything was so clean and luxurious. He took his time and washed his body very clean. He had not taken any shower for at least two weeks. He enjoyed this opportunity so much. He felt that he was in heaven. After he finished, he cleaned the bathroom and tried to leave it the same way he found it originally.

He then came into the bedroom where the old man took him. He saw a photo of a young man on the top of the clothes chest. He knew this young man must be his son or someone very close to the old man. Daniel went to bed. He had not been in such a good and comfortable bed for a long time. He fell asleep very quickly and soundly.

He woke up around 8 o'clock in the morning, Christmas day. He noticed that the old man was still sleeping. He walked downstairs very quietly. He entered the kitchen. He found the espresso machine and some coffee. He wanted to get everything ready so when the old man woke up, he would prepare him a nice cup of espresso to show his appreciation for allowing him to stay in his apartment last night. He also found some eggs and ham in the refrigerator.

When he was preparing these, he heard the old man's steps coming down the stairs. He came out of kitchen,

"Good morning, sir! I hope you feel better this morning."

It took the old man a few moments to orient himself. At first, he was wondered who this young man was, where had he come from, and what was he doing in his home. After a while, he began to remember what had happened last night. He was so drunk last night, and this young man might have just saved him from getting sick or death.

"I feel better now. Did you sleep good?"

"Yes, sir! The best sleep in the last 6 years."

"Why 6 years?" The old man asked curiously.

Then, Daniel introduced himself and told the old man about his dream of chasing the sun and how much suffering he had encountered. To the old man, this was just like a story shown only in movies. He had never believed that there was someone else who was less lucky than him. The old man began thinking deeply and recalled his past couple of years. Daniel turned the espresso machine on and began to cook some eggs and ham. He also found some bread on the kitchen counter. In a few minutes, he poured a cup of espresso for the old man and prepared some warm breakfast for him.

"Sit down and eat with me. I have not had any companionship for a while."

He sat down on the other side of small dining table where the old man's son used to sit. When the old man looked at him, his eyes turned red,

"My son used to sit there and talk to me."

"You son? The photo in the bedroom?"

The old man nodded his head.

"Is he away?"

"No! He is dead. He killed himself." The old man said and couldn't help the tears in his eyes.

Then, the old man told him the story.

The old man's name was Diego Vega and he was 64 years old. He established an import and export company, Vega Trading, Inc., when he was 30 years old. He got married when he was 35 years old with a lady, Anna, who was 25 years old. They always hoped to have a child. However, it was not until he was 45 years old that his wife became pregnant. She birthed a son and they named him Rogelio. They were very happy. Mr. Vega was keeping himself in the business he created and became very successful. His business was especially great when Communist China opened their gate to the western world in 1973. He grabbed the opportunity and since then the business kept growing and growing.

Unfortunately, three years ago, when his wife, Anna, was 51 years old, she suddenly passed away with stomach cancer. When this happened, his son, Rogelio, was only 16 years old. This was a big shock to the family. However, Mr. Vega could not spend time both for his son and the business equally. Furthermore, he just could not face the cruelty of his wife's death. He was deeply in love with his wife. He didn't realize that his son would need him more than ever because of his wife's death. He lived in sorrow and felt pity for himself. He just didn't understand why his destiny would fool him like this. His business began to go down due to lack of his attention and enthusiasm. At the same time, his son would hang around with bad friends.

He remembered that a few days before last Christmas, his son came home very upset. At the same time, he also received a notice from Rogelio's schoolteacher that his son might be delayed for high school graduation for another year due to poor grades. When his Rogelio arrived home, Mr. Vega shouted at him about his school without knowing his son was upset due to a huge fight with his girlfriend. He remembered he called his son a failure and a disgrace to the family. He had a fight with his son. After the fight, he left home to the bar looking for some place to calm down. When he returned to his apartment, he noticed that the water from the bathroom was running down through the stairs. He went into the bathroom and saw his son's dead body with blood gushing from his left wrist. Rogelio had committed suicide. This was a shock that hit him even harder than his wife's death. He believed that it was his fault that he hadn't concerned himself with his son's feeling about his mother's death. He had lost the meaning of his life. All of the wealth he had earned didn't mean anything to him now.

"He was only 18 years old." Diego said with tears in his eyes.

It had been a year since the tragedy. He almost completely ignored his business and got drunk often. Though he had a sister, named Dominga, she married a French professor, Henry Petitfour, and lived in Paris. The number of his employees had decreased from 12 to only 5. If he didn't find the way to correct this downward spiral, he would soon face bankruptcy. Last night, Christmas Eve; was the darkest day of his life. He missed his wife and his son. He went out and got drunk. Usually, he had a maid, Elena, come to help him clean the apartment and wash the laundry every day. She also cooked for him often. However, due to the holiday, she and her daughter, Belicia, went to southern Spain to see her Mom and celebrate Christmas with her family. Diego's sister's family couldn't come to see him this Christmas due to Henry's mother's critical health condition.

When he finished his story, he looked at Daniel,

"I have not thanked you for your help last night. You are a good young man."

"I feel very sorry for you, sir! I wish I could help you more."

"Why don't you stay until my maid comes back? I will enjoy your company very much. You remind me of my son."

"Really? It will be so great for me! It's so cold sleeping in the street; especially during the winter time." Daniel looked at Diego with such appreciation.

Since Diego had closed his company until January 2, he had plenty of time. He thought he would be alone by himself for the next 7 days.

In the following six days, he began to know Daniel better. Daniel cooked for him, cleaned his apartment, and washed his laundry. When he had time, he continued his studies in Spanish language. When he had questions, he asked Diego to help him. They ate, played chess, watched TV, and went to shop together. In just a couple days, Diego began to smile which he had lost for more than a year. He asked Daniel to use all his son's belongings like his clothes, music sound system, and even a small TV. When Diego preferred to be alone, Daniel had his own world in his room. Daniel took care of Diego very thoroughly. During these few days, Diego acknowledged that Daniel was not just a good-looking young man, but also a smart and quick learner. He began to explain to him how business worked, how to manage it, budget control, and how to handle accounting.

After nearly 7 days of living together, Diego had a strong feeling that Daniel was just like his own son. It seemed that Daniel had filled up his emotional void he had lost for a year. At the same time, Daniel knew that, tomorrow, January 2, the maid would return. That implied that he must again face his destiny and return to life in the streets. He felt sad to leave since, for 7 days, Diego was not only like his father, but also a teacher, and a friend. Daniel knew he would miss him very much. Though he wished he could stay, he didn't expect this kind of luxury to remain forever. He just appreciated what he had had for the last 7 days. During their dinner on January 1, Diego poured two glasses of wine and gave one to Daniel.

"Happy New Year, Daniel! Thank you for keeping me company these past 7 days."

"Happy New Year, sir!" When Daniel said this, the tears came spontaneously. Diego sensed that Daniel was very emotional about his departure the following morning.

"Daniel, would you like to work for me?"

Daniel was surprised by the question. He didn't expect this, and his tears just poured out. He looked at Diego,

"I don't know what to say, sir! You have treated me so nice and kind." He nodded his head and said, "Yes, I would like to work for you, sir.".

"I will show you the company's warehouse and introduce you to all the employees tomorrow morning. You will begin from the most basic discipline in the business."

"Naturally, sir! Anything is better than begging on the street."

"Yes! You can stay here temporarily. Furthermore, I like your companionship, Daniel."

* * *

The following morning, Tuesday, Daniel woke up earlier than usual. He had a job today. For 6 years, he felt he had lost the sun he was chasing. Now, he saw the sunlight again. He was sincerely excited. He wanted to catch and embrace this sun and would not lose it again. He now had a renewed hope for his life.

Diego woke up early as well. His working spirit had returned. He had lost this spirit and inspiration for a long time. Somehow, he felt that Daniel had offered him a great deal of comfort and new hope for his company.

After breakfast, they took a taxi to Vega Trading, Inc. that was located near the suburb of Madrid. They went inside a building. This was the first time that Diego had gone to his company on time for nearly a year.

When they entered his office, Diego saw his secretary was there.

"Happy new year, Solana!"

When Solana saw him walk in with Daniel, she was so surprised.

"Happy New Year to you, too! Mr. Vega. You are early today. Have not seen you come here so early for a long time." She was so happy to see that Diego had a good mood and looked happy again.

"Oh! Ya! Solana! This is Daniel. He will work for me from today. Yes! Can you also call for a meeting for everyone at 9:00 a.m.?"

"Of course! Mr. Vega."

Diego then took Daniel to all the offices and explained to him what kind of job each office handled. He could see that some employees had not arrived at work yet. He knew this was because he himself was always late during the past year. Consequently, all employees didn't care too much about punctuality. Diego knew that leaders lead best by example and understood that he had not set the appropriate tone for the company. This was all changing now. Diego then took Daniel to the warehouse located at the rear side of the building. He explained to him different areas of goods and from where they were imported.

"This area is the biggest mess in the last few years. Everything is disordered now. Your first job is to keep this place clean and organized. Though the job is the most basic, however, it is the most important. Furthermore, it would help you understand the goods we import."

"Yes, sir! I will do my best."

At 9 o'clock, everyone, total of 7 including Diego and Daniel, was in the company's conference room. Some of them felt bad when they came in late and knew Diego was already there. After everyone sat down and settled,

"Good morning! First! I would like to wish you and your families a Happy New Year." Diego showed a smile which his employees had not seen for a long time. They knew that it was a new year and it seemed that Mr. Vega's motivation in business had returned.

"Happy New Year to you, sir!" They all said.

"I want to tell you that I will be here on time every day starting from today. I feel it is time to pick up some business that we left behind these last couple of years. In addition, I would like to introduce a new employee of the company, Mr. Daniel Eraclid. He will be working in the warehouse to re-organize the entire stock we have. Ciro! I need you to cooperate with him fully and give him the stock inventory today. I would like to talk to all of you individually today to clearly understand the company's current situation. Solana will arrange the meeting schedules with you. If you need to leave this area, please let her know first. Paco! You are the manager in this company; I would like to talk to you first. How about 10 o'clock this morning in my office?"

"Yes! Mr. Vega! I will prepare for it." Paco said. Paco had been working for him for nearly 15 years. Diego trusted him more than anyone else. Paco had been worried about the future of the company since Diego's wife and son's death. He believed the company would face bankruptcy in just a couple years. He was so happy to see that Diego's spirit had returned. At the same time, "Who is this young man next to him? What is their relationship?" He wondered. In the past, before Diego hired or fired any employee, he always had consulted with him first.

When the meeting was over, he asked Ciro to explain all about the company's inventory to Daniel. Daniel had some difficulty understanding the Spanish. He had many questions but didn't know how to ask. He was a little bit worried that he might not be able to handle the job Mr. Vega wished.

Diego returned to his office with his secretary after the meeting.

"Solana! I need you to contact our immigration attorney as soon as you can. I want to hire Daniel, but he doesn't have any identity. He came from Romania."

"Yes! I will take care of it today."

"By the way, please keep all of this between you and me." Diego said. He didn't want any employee to know about Daniel's background. This might cause them to despise him.

At 10:00 AM, Paco reported to Diego. He gave Diego a detailed report about last year's business. Diego started to realize that his business was near the edge of bankruptcy. He was glad that he began to pay attention to it again, otherwise, the consequences could not be imaginable. Deep in his heart, he knew that it was Daniel who saved him and his company from going down. If he hadn't encountered Daniel, he wouldn't have the same feeling he now had, the feeling of hope and the energy required to do the work to remain successful in business.

After he met all the other four employees, his mind was much clearer about the entire company. He began to dig out the list of his suppliers and customers. He spent the whole afternoon pondering a new plan and strategies for Vega Trading, Inc. He knew that he needed to travel to India, Thailand, and China again. He needed to know their new products. He must also know what his retail customers wanted.

Diego asked Solana to order two lunches for him and Daniel since all employees brought their lunch usually. They ate in Diego's office,

"Daniel, Do you have a good idea about inventory yet?"

"I am sorry to say, not too much yet. I am learning. There are too many things I need to learn. Oh! Yes, sir! I would like to stay a little bit longer today to clear some questions I had. Would you mind going home first?"

"Not at all!" Diego replied and took some money from his pocket and gave it to Daniel. He knew that Daniel didn't have any money yet.

"Take a taxi! It would be faster." Diego was very happy to see his enthusiasm for learning.

"Thank you, sir!"

Daniel stayed until almost 9:00 PM. He took the subway to get home. When he arrived, it was 9:45 PM. He rang the bell; a lady came to open it.

"You must be Daniel. I am Elena. I am Mr. Vega's maid." She said.

"Nice to meet you." Daniel said and bowed to her.

After he went in, she said,

"I must go back to my apartment now. It's too late for me. Take care of yourself. Dinner is on the table." She left quickly with her coat.

When Daniel entered, he saw Diego was sitting in front of his desk and working. He knew he must have had a busy and tough day.

"Good evening, sir. I am back."

"Yes! I heard the bell. Please, go eat dinner and rest. Wait! How much do you know about computers?"

"I don't know anything about computers, sir! I am sorry."

"OK! You have to learn some basic computer program and its function for business. I will ask Paco to teach you tomorrow. Now, go eat. You must be hungry."

Daniel felt so warm. Nobody had ever been concerned about him so nicely in the last 6 years. He bowed to Diego and entered the kitchen. Dinner was still warm. It seemed that Diego had waited for him for some time and had just finished his dinner not too long ago. It was a very nice dinner cooked by Elena. Comparing the cooking he did for Mr. Vega the last few days, this was definitely much better.

After dinner, he took a shower and then sat down to write a letter to his Mom. He had not written home for a while now. He knew that his Mom worried about him very much. Now that he had a definite address, his Mom would be able to write him back. The last time he received his Mom's letter was a year ago when he stayed with the Italian gangster family, New Heaven. He told his Mom that he found a good job and was learning how to run a business. He also mentioned that he hoped to send some money home soon. After that, he came downstairs and saw Mr. Diego was still working. He didn't disturb him and went to bed.

The next day, Diego asked Paco to teach Daniel how to use the computer for business, inventory control, and accounting. In addition, Daniel also continued his duty taking care of the warehouse inventory. In just a couple of weeks, the warehouse had a new look. At the same time, Daniel also received a letter from his father. Inside the letter was a family photo. He was so happy and saw all his brothers and sisters were grown up. He felt so good and prayed to God for his mercy and kindness.

He spent nearly two weeks re-organizing the arrangement of inventory in the warehouse. It was more efficient now and the goods could be protected better until they reached customers' hands. When all the employees saw Mr. Vega and Daniel's working attitude, they also changed and were motivated. In a month or so, most of the old

Vega Trading Inc. customers returned to them. Since Diego had not taken care of business for a couple years and there were not too many new products, many customers had switched their suppliers. Now, the business had resumed to about 70% of what it used to be a year ago. The best news for Daniel was Mr. Vega told him that his immigration attorney was able to get an ID card for him so he could stay in Spain legally. When he heard this, he couldn't restrain his emotions. He cried openly right in front of Mr. Vega. Diego knew that this was because of his gratitude and happiness.

At the end of the month, Daniel received his first paycheck, an amount of 130,000 pesetas that was equivalent to US$850. After he received the check, he went to his small office in the corner of warehouse and wept freely. This was the biggest amount of money he had earned in his life. At noontime the following day, he took the check to open an account. After that, he purchased a bank draft of US$500 and sent it home. Other than the bank draft, he also included in the letter a photo of him working in the warehouse. He felt that his life was so beautiful, and he was so fortunate. He knew that there were still thousands of 'sun chasers' on the street of the western countries searching for the sun.

After that initial paycheck, Daniel kept sending money home each month. From the letter he received, he knew that the money he sent had changed the entire family's life. The average income of a Romania engineer was only about US$100 per month at that time.

5
NEW LIFE

Nearly one year had passed and Mr. Vega had never mentioned that he wanted Daniel to leave his apartment. Actually, he could feel that Mr. Vega had treated him like his own son. Often, they chatted and laughed. They talked about the company and how to improve the business. From Daniel, Mr. Vega also realized how difficult it was for any civilian to survive in eastern European countries.

Another Christmas Eve arrived. The company was closed from Christmas Eve to New Year's Day. After their Christmas Eve dinner, Daniel told Diego that he would like to take a walk and then he left. He walked back to the street where he met Diego the first time, the Christmas Eve of last year. Like the previous year, the street was almost empty. Though it was not raining or snowing this time, the weather was still very cold. He sat at the spot where Diego fell last year speechless. When he thought of his past and the Christmas Eve a year ago, he couldn't help but to begin to cry. About 20 minutes or so later, he heard some steps approaching and saw Mr. Vega came there too having realized that Daniel was also there. The old man looked at Daniel and couldn't keep his emotion contained. He stepped forward and hugged Daniel tightly. His eyes were red and tearing. Both of them appreciated the special moment of meeting in this place exactly a year ago. Their feelings superseded that of a boss and an employee. They felt like father and son.

Two days later, the family of Diego's only sister, Dominga, returned to Madrid to visit him. Diego was very excited. He had not seen his sister and her family for a few years. Dominga was his baby sister. Between Diego and Dominga, there was 13 years age difference. His sister had two children, a girl, Nina, and a boy, Amato. Three years ago, after his wife's funeral, Henry took the family back to Paris due to his professor job. "It's been three years already. I last saw them at Anna's funeral." He thought. He also remembered that before they moved, both his and his sister's family always got together and had a very good time. All three kids could get along with each other sweetly. He remembered that his son, Rogelio, was 16, Nina was also 16, and Amato was only 13 years old. He smiled when he thought of this.

From the expression on Diego's face, Daniel could see how excited and how much anxiety Diego felt about seeing his sister and her family again. He missed them very much. After dinner, he sat in the living room quietly and took a look at the clock on the wall. "Why were they so late? They should be here by now. It's 7:30 already." He thought.

"Daniel, are all of the rooms ready for them?" He asked Daniel who was studying English from a book. After one year of working, Daniel believed if he wanted to have contact with customers other than just Spanish ones, he must learn English. In his mind, Diego's business should be able to reach the entire European market instead of just Spain.

"Yes! sir! Amato will share the room with me. Nina has her own room. And Mr. Petitfour and his wife will use the guest room. Right?"

"Yes! It is correct. You did it well, Daniel."

While they were talking, the doorbell rang. Diego stood up excited and smiling.

"They are here! Daniel, open the door for me."

"Yes, sir!" He went to the door and opened it. "Welcome back." He said.

"You must be Daniel. Diego talked about you a few times on the phone. Nice to meet you." Dominga said. She then introduced Henry, Amato, and Nina to him while they were entering the door. Diego had already been standing at the door of the living room waiting for them. When Dominga saw him, she could see that though Diego was older he still had a strong spirit.

"Hi! Diego! Good to see you again."

Diego stepped forward to hug her tightly and his eyes turning red. Henry, Amato, and Nina also came forward to hug him. When they went into the living room,

"Diego! I am sorry that we were late. You know, there were a lot of travelers during this time of the year.

While they were talking, Daniel went into the kitchen to warm up the food. Dinner was ready for them an hour ago, but it was cold now. Since the maid was not there during this time of the year, Daniel tried to cook his best dishes he had learned from the maid, Elena. He always participated in Elena's cooking on weekends for the past year. He enjoyed cooking very much. Half an hour later, dinner was ready. The good tasty aromas of food wafted through the hallway and entered the living room.

"Smells so good. I am hungry." Amato said.

"He is always hungry." Dominga said. Everyone laughed while Daniel stepped in and said,

"Dinner is ready."

They had to eat in the dining room today. The dining table in the kitchen where Diego and Daniel used to eat was too small for so many people. Diego remembered that the last time they used this dining room was more than three years ago. He felt so happy. After dinner,

"Everything is very delicious. Daniel, you are a very good cook!" Nina complimented.

Daniel just smiled at her and felt she was so beautiful and elegant. "She is a lady with high education." He thought. Then, he thought of himself. He became so humble right in front of her. After dinner, they chatted about the past. Daniel just listened and answered any question she had. He was just like a good schoolboy in the classroom.

That evening, Daniel slept on the floor and gave the bed to Amato. Though Amato resisted, he insisted. Just in a couple days, they became two good friends. He was 23 years old and Amato was only 17. Amato loved to listen to his story of chasing the sun. To him, this was a very intriguing and the most amazing story he had ever heard. Daniel just avoided talking about being sexual abused. Amato was too young to know and understand the cruelty and the ugliness of the real world.

They stayed until December 31st, right after lunch, when they had to return to Paris for Henry's work. When Diego hugged them and said goodbye, again, he couldn't help that he cried.

"Diego! Take care of yourself. Henry said he wanted to retire in another three years. After retirement, he liked to move back to Madrid forever."

"Don't wait for three years. Come back to see me every year. I miss you a lot."

"We'll see if we can come back again soon."

They left with a taxi to the airport. After they left, Diego sat in the living room and recalled all of the good times he had the past few days. "I have not been so happy for more than three years now." He thought. When he was sitting there, he saw Daniel's English book was there. He took a look and realized that Daniel tried to learn English by himself.

Half an hour later, Daniel finished his cleaning in the kitchen and came in to the living room.

"Do you like to learn?"

"Yes, sir! I didn't even finish high school. I ran away in the last year of high school. I wish I could be educated." He thought of Amato and Nina, well educated. He felt so inadequate intellectually.

"What would you say if I sent you to a professional business school. You may learn anything related to business such as business planning and management, financial planning, computers, and English."

Daniel looked at Diego with shock. He would never have imagined that he could go back to school again. He was very confident that after a whole year of learning Spanish, he could handle it well.

"It will be so great! I want to be educated." He said.

On February 15, Diego registered him to enter a well-known professional school in Madrid, IE Business School. This school specialized in business creation and management. He would go to school until 2:30 PM and then immediately went to work. He usually worked until 9 o'clock in the evening. When he had time, he would use it for studying. In the beginning, Daniel had a hard time to catch up to his classmates. However, only after 3 months, he was already at the top one third of the class.

When Diego saw this, he was very happy. He believed that Daniel would be a big asset for Viega Trading, Inc. He liked him like his own son and treated him like one as well.

* * *

Romania Home Reunion

The semester finished. Daniel had learned so much and received a very high grade that made his schoolteacher, Mr. Juan Dominguez, very surprised. When he called Diego and gave a compliment to Daniel, Diego was so happy. Summer time had come, and school was closed for two months. Daniel had something on his mind. For a few days, he was very quiet and didn't know if he should ask Mr. Vega.

Diego could sense the change. One evening, after dinner, while they were sitting in the living room,

"You have been so quiet for a few days now. Is there anything bothering you?"

"No, sir! I am just homesick. I miss my family. I have not seen them for over seven years."

"Why don't you take a few days off and go see them? I believe that you should go. I couldn't imagine how much your parents must miss you."

"Really?" Daniel jumped out of his chair.

Diego could see how happy Daniel was when he heard his suggestion.

"I will call my travel agent and get a ticket for you. Now, tell me where exactly your home was. I need to know so I can book a ticket landing in the airport which is close to your home."

"My home is in a small town called Turda near the city, Cluj-Napoca." Daniel replied.

The next morning, Diego asked his secretary to book an airplane ticket for Daniel. Daniel would leave on Friday and return on Monday two weeks later. Since Daniel had become a crucial key person working in the company, Diego didn't want him away too long.

When Diego gave him the airplane ticket, Daniel realized that it was true that he was really going home to see his family.

He wrote a letter to his parents first about the news. There was still no telephone installed in his home yet. At night, he went out to buy some gifts for his parents, and his elder brother and younger sisters. He also took half of his savings from the bank he had saved for one and a half years, totaling 800,000 pesetas that was equivalent to US$5,000 dollars. He also brought US$1,500 with him if he needed it. He would have more if he didn't send home money almost every month. He believed that he would not need this money since he didn't have to worry about food and living staying with Diego. He knew his family would need this money more than he did.

He was so excited like a child waiting for Christmas' arrival. During the following two weeks, Daniel worked very hard and tried to arrange all of the work so he could be two weeks ahead of schedule.

On Friday, June 27, 1997, he arrived at the Cluj-Napoca airport. This was the first time he experienced flying. When he arrived, his father hired a taxi to pick him up. His youngest sister, Cristina, also came. His mother and grandma were home preparing a feast for dinner. His elder brother, Florin, was still in the army and would come home tomorrow while his other sister, Danisa, had to work today.

When Daniel exited through the arrival passage hall, his eyes were all red and filling with tears. He had mixed feelings of happiness and sadness when he thought of the past seven years and now seeing his family. He saw his father and a lady who waved hands at him.

"Papa. I am so sorry and so happy to see you." He could not help his tears from rushing out. He was so happy. He couldn't continue talking and just hugged his father tightly for a long minute.

"Daniel, you have grown up." His father said. He also could not stop his tears from coming. After a minute or so, his father pushed him apart,

"Let's me take a look of you. Daniel. Seven long years." He changed into smiles and laughing. Daniel noticed the lady next to his father; he recognized that she was his youngest sister, Cristina, 17 years old already. When he left home, she was only 10 years old.

"Hi, Christina. You are a lady now." Daniel hugged her tightly. He remembered that before he left home, Christina always liked to follow him everywhere and asked questions. "What is the difference today?" Daniel sighed.

"This is for you, Daniel. Welcome home. I missed you. We all missed you." Christina said and gave him a bunch of red roses from their garden.

They entered the taxi and left the airport. When the car passed through the city Cluj-Napoca, his eyes were red. He couldn't believe that he would have returned to Romania. He came to Cluj-Napoca a few times with his father to purchase some equipment before. Some buildings were so familiar and many new buildings were built. He couldn't believe how much change had happened during the last seven years. However, when the car entered the town of Turda, it seemed to have remained exactly the same as before. The car passed through his high school where he and two other good friends were talking about running away. It seemed that everything was just like yesterday.

When he arrived, he saw his grandma was waiting outside of the house. Nobody knew when Daniel would arrive. Daniel's mom was in the kitchen preparing a big dinner to welcome Daniel's return tonight. When his grandma saw the taxi, she had already suspected that this taxi was Daniel's since there was nobody who would hire a taxi in Turda. It was just too expensive for them. When Daniel saw his grandma waiting outside of the house, tears poured out from his eyes. He knew his grandma must have been waiting there for a long time. Actually, he believed that she might not even have had a good night's sleep since knowing Daniel was coming home. Daniel was the second born in his generation. His grandma loved him more than anything or anyone else. When his grandma knew Daniel ran away seven years ago, she cried for a whole month.

Daniel opened the taxi door and rushed to his grandma while his father was paying the taxi driver and took his luggage out.

"Grandma! I missed you a lot." Daniel couldn't help all of the tears that he shed when he hugged his grandma. He could feel his grandma's body was shivering due to the excitement. She looked at Daniel and couldn't speak a word. She rose up her right hand and caressed Daniel's face as she used to. Finally, she couldn't help the tears from her eyes. She cried aloud. She needed to cry out all of the lost feelings she had held deep in her heart for the last seven years. "Seven years. Grandma is older now. She is 73 years old already." When he thought of this, he hugged his grandma even tighter.

After a few minutes, she stopped her crying and began to laugh. She just could not believe that she would see Daniel again. They went in the house with Daniel's luggage. His Mom came out of the kitchen. When she saw Daniel, she couldn't help crying out loudly. This was the release of missing, worry, and joy.

"Thank God! It is true that you are home."

"Mom! I am sorry. I let you worry about me." Daniel hugged his Mom and the tears started all over again.

"Let me take a look at you." She just could not believe her eyes that Daniel was there. "You have grown up." Mom said. She kept touching him to make sure it was really him.

"Mom! It's been seven years already."

They talked a little bit and then his grandma and Mom went into the kitchen to prepare dinner.

"Your sister, Danisa, should be home soon. She is 21 now and working in Cluj-Napoca." His father said.

While they were talking, Danisa walked in and saw Daniel. It felt a little bit strange that both of them had grown up and were adults now.

"Hi, Danisa. You have grown up. When I left, you were 13, no, 14 right?" Daniel hugged her.

Dinner was ready in half an hour. They all sat down around the dining table. The table was full of all the food that Daniel loved when he was a child. His elder brother, Florin, was the only one missing. He would return tomorrow.

"Papa! Mama! I am sorry that I ran away. I miss home very much."

"It's OK, as long as you are safe and happy. It's OK."

His parents began to ask him about his life in the last seven years. Daniel just didn't have the heart to tell them the complete truth that he had been seriously abused and how much suffering he actually had experienced. He just told them he found miscellaneous jobs here and there and could not earn enough money so he could send some home. It was not until last year, when he found this job in Madrid and how Diego took care of him. While he spoke, his grandmother who knew him best sensed that there was more to Daniel's tale than what he shared. Her wisdom knew that he had suffered, but she respected his privacy and did not challenge his stories. Her heart just poured out to embrace her grandson and prayed for his well-being and prosperous future.

They had a very nice dinner. This had reminded Daniel of the past when he was a child at home. His mother's cooking, though not the best in the world, was different and special. It had an important ingredient other cooking had not had, the ingredient of love.

* * *

The next day, Daniel went to visit the home of his best friend, Jean Aron. He was so anxious to know if his parents had had any news about him. When he arrived at Jean's home, he was so surprised to see Jean there getting ready to go to the field to work. When they saw each other, both stared at the other for a few seconds,

"Hey! Jean! It's been such a long time. We have not seen each other for 6 years." Daniel said.

"Hi! Daniel, I didn't know you were home!" Daniel's appearance reminded him of how much suffering they had experienced when they were in West Germany together with Anton.

"How have you been?" Daniel asked with concern.

"After we separated, I stayed in Germany for another six months, I felt very depressed and decided to come back. Now, I am working for my Dad."

"Do you have any news from Anton? Is he OK? Did he also return home?"

"No, Daniel. As far as I know, there was no news about him. His parents came to ask me a few times, too. I felt so sorry for them. I just didn't know how to tell them. Their hearts were broken. Anton was always a shy boy. His parents missed him so much."

"There were no letters from him?"

"No! He simply disappeared. Nobody knows where he is and how he is."

"I want to visit his parents later. Do you want to go with me?"

"No, Daniel. I am very afraid to see them. Whenever I saw them, I felt so sad. I felt that it was my responsibility. My fault. We shouldn't have run away seven years ago. I am sorry, Daniel. I shouldn't have convinced you to run away with me."

"No! No! Don't say that. It's not your fault. It was our dream, remember? Our dream! Let's get together sometimes. I will be here until next weekend."

"What! You are going away again? I thought you had come home to stay."

"No! I am just visiting. I am working in Madrid now. I have a job there."

"That means you have found your sun."

"Yes! I found it, but I don't have it yet. I must go back and work harder so I can grasp it in my hands."

"Congratulation! You had better luck than me."

"Here! Please, take this, Jean. I hope this will help you somehow." Daniel gave him US$500. This was a considerable amount of money in Romania in 1997.

"Thank you very much!" Jean took the money with appreciation. He felt that perhaps he shouldn't have returned. Had he endured a little longer, maybe Jean would have found his own sun the way it seemed that Daniel had finally found his.

After Daniel left Jean, he walked to Anton's home. It took him only 30 minutes or so to walk there. The town was small, and one could walk almost everywhere without needing a car. When he arrived at Anton's home, Anton's grandparents and his Mom were there. When he entered the door, they were so surprised to see Daniel. They knew Daniel pretty well since Anton, Jean, and Daniel were very good friends and always played together.

"Mrs. Joldea. How are you doing? Do you have any news from Anton?" Daniel asked without too much expectation of a positive response. He already knew about the situation from Jean half an hour earlier.

Anton's Mom was shocked to see Daniel. She paused for a moment with tears in her eyes,

"No, Daniel. There is no news. It has been seven years now. Do you know where and how is he? I have been very worried about him." Anton's Mom asked anxiously. Anton's grandparents were just sitting there unable to utter a word. They were so sad and had lost hope about Anton.

"I am sorry, Mrs. Joldea. I have not had contact with him since we separated more than 6 years ago." Daniel replied sadly. He knew that since Anton was the only boy in his family, he must have broken his family's heart.

Daniel did not have any words to comfort Anton's Mom. However, he looked at her and said,

"Mrs. Joldea. I will find him. I swear I will spend my remaining lifetime to find him." Daniel stepped forward and held her hands and, at the same time, gave her US$500. That was all he could do to help them. He couldn't stay longer because the sorrow in Anton's home was overwhelming.

Anton's Mom just looked at Daniel through her tears.

"Please, please, Daniel. Please find my Anton."

With a profound feeling of sadness, Daniel walked to the high school where the three of them used to be together. He sat there for a long time. He thought of the past, the present, and the coming future. He sat there and watched a new generation of students, 14-16 years old, playing in the field.

That evening, his brother, Florin came home. Daniel was always a little afraid of his older brother mixed with some feeling of respect. After all, Florin was the oldest child in the family. In order to help his family's financial situation, he sacrificed himself and joined the army.

When they met before dinner, Daniel saw his brother walk into the house wearing his military uniform,

"Hi! Florin!" Daniel did not know what to say exactly. It seemed the distance between he and his brother had increased further. However, his brother stepped forward surprising Daniel and said,

"Welcome home, Daniel. I am so glad you are home." He hugged Daniel tightly with sincere concern. Daniel now realized for the first time that his brother seemed so solemn and serious before because he hid his emotions deeply inside of him. Florin's greeting made Daniel feel warm and welcomed.

Daniel had a great time on this trip. He visited Jean a couple times more. However, they were not 16 years old anymore and now had to face the reality of life. Right before his departure, he went to see Anton's parents again and told them that he would try hard to find Anton though he did not know how. He also installed a telephone in his parents' home. He and the entire family were so happy about this because they would now be able to talk to each other whenever they needed.

He returned to Madrid with mixed feelings of joy, sadness, and loss. Time passed so fast, it had been 7 years.

Travel Together

Due to the increased opening of eastern European borders and China, the import and export business grew rapidly. In just a couple of years, business growth had accelerated rapidly. Diego's company, Vega Trading, Inc. had doubled its growth and the number of employees increased to 12.

"Daniel. I think we need more contacts and suppliers of goods in China, Thailand, and India. We also need more variety of new and good supplies from the East." Diego said one morning.

"Sir, I also thought of this a couple of weeks ago and wanted to see if I could find an opportunity to talk to you about this." Daniel replied.

"I plan to travel to China, India, and Thailand soon. I would like you to go with me. You know, to have some experience and meet new suppliers. Furthermore, I am 67 years old now and long travels alone would be more tiring for me. The only concern is that you are the key person here. If both of us leave together, the company may become chaotic."

Daniel replied, "Mr. Vega! I believe Paco would be able to handle it. He is the most senior employee and a responsible man. If we go for a couple weeks, I believe that he could handle the business competently."

"OK, in this case, we should leave the 2nd week of August. This will allow us to see the goods, make appropriate decisions, sign pertinent contracts with suppliers, and bring the goods in. We need to get ready for Christmas time. You know, Christmas time has reliably brought us more than one third of the entire year's business. Furthermore, we need to return by the end of August for your school. Classes start at the beginning of September, isn't that correct?"

"Yes, Mr. Vega. I will prepare everything to get ready for this trip." Daniel replied.

After nearly 3 years of working for Diego, Daniel had become Diego's right-hand man, but also like his son actually. In a practical sense, Daniel had complete authority to manage the company. Diego had become a consultant and adviser to the company. Because Daniel had a steady job, he received his Spanish citizenship without any problem. He now needed to apply for his Spanish passport which usually took a week to process.

Since Daniel had never traveled to the East and had no experience in business negotiation, Diego believed he should go to handle this aspect of the business himself and also use it as an opportunity to teach Daniel some critical negotiation; especially with Eastern companies.

On Friday, August 14th, 1998, they were on their way to Asia. This was the first time Daniel experienced a long journey; especially to the mysterious Asian countries. All he knew about these countries was from books. He was very excited; especially because he would be together with Diego. He felt Diego was just like his father. They planned to return to Madrid on the 28th of August which just gave Daniel enough time to prepare for his last year of business school.

They went to Shanghai, China first. Shanghai was a commercial business city, the gate to enter Chinese culture. They were very successful in building relations with 10 supply companies. They were very happy about this success. They spent 7 days in China. Other than their business dealings, they also took a tour to visit well-known sights around Shanghai.

Next, they went to Bangkok, Thailand and spent three days to establish another 4 connections. Once the contracts were signed, they flew to New Delhi, India which was the final stop in their travels. When they arrived, it was rainy season and it rained every day. As a result of the constant rain, they arranged some business meetings with various suppliers in their hotel. Though they did not have an opportunity to see their factories personally, Diego and Daniel got a clear sense of the quality of the goods from the samples the suppliers brought. They signed contractual agreements with two of the export companies.

All in all, it was a greatly successful business trip. Both of them enjoyed the trip. They departed New Delhi on August 28th of 1998. Due to heavy rain, the airplane was delayed for nearly one hour. When they arrived at Rome to transfer airplanes, they had only 25 minutes to reach the other gate.

"We must hurry, otherwise, we will miss our connection." Diego said once he stepped out of the airplane.

"Yes, Mr. Vega." Daniel took Diego's handbags and both of them ran to another terminal. Only 10 minutes or so later, Diego was in distress.

"Daniel, I can't breathe! My left chest has sharp pain." Diego slowed down and puffed. His face was pale, and his body was drenched in a cold sweat. Finally, he stopped and sat on a chair nearby.

Daniel was so worried about the situation.

"Should I call for help?" Daniel asked.

"Wait for a few minutes to see if I feel better." Diego replied.

After 10 minutes, Diego caught his breath again and his pallor had completely waned. His face looked normal.

"Let's go slower. If we miss the flight, we will take the next one." Diego said.

Slowly, they arrived at the new gate and realized that their departure flight had been delayed due to the airplane's late arrival. Actually, they realized they did not have to run and had plenty of time to transfer.

When they returned to Madrid, Daniel arranged an urgent appointment the next day with a well-known cardiac specialist for Diego. After his medical evaluation the next day, they received the report from the Doctor that Diego needed an angioplasty procedure as soon as possible.

The third day after their return, Diego had the surgery. It was a complete success. The Doctor believed that they found the problem early. If treatment had been delayed, the prognosis would have been grave. When Diego was in the recovery room, he thought,

"I am only 67 and I have already had a serious heart problem. What will happen if I die?" Diego sighed. This thought preoccupied his mind.

Daniel came to see Diego every day and updated him about the company. This was especially important because all the new orders for goods would arrive in a couple weeks. They needed to organize everything and a new warehouse. A week later, Diego was medically cleared and returned to his home. He was recovering very fast.

Only two months after they returned from Asia, the order volume increased by double what they anticipated. This was being driven by the new products with decent prices. Especially with only a couple of months before Christmas, they needed to hire more temporary helpers to successfully manage the new demand. All of these developments made Diego very happy. However, deep in his heart, there was a shadow hanging around that he could not get rid of.

As in the past two years, Diego's sister and her family, Henry, Nina, and Amato came to have a reunion with Diego during Christmas time. For Diego, it was a mixture of joy and sadness. He was definitely happy about the family reunion and the success of business. However, at the same time, he worried about his health.

Adoption

On August 10 of 1998, during lunch break, Diego asked Daniel if he would like to take a walk in the nearby park with him. This had happened a few times already in the past. Whenever Diego had some important business to discuss with Daniel, he always asked Daniel to take a walk with him in the park. They could discuss freely, and Daniel could always offer his opinion or advice to Diego. After more than three years of relationship, Daniel was not just a valuable company employee; he was literally like Diego's son. When they sat down on the park bench, Diego looked directly into Daniel's eyes and said,

"Daniel, I have a serious question to ask you. I pray you give me an honest answer."

Daniel thought there was some serious problem in the company that had bothered Diego.

"Is there any problem in the company, Mr. Vega?" Daniel asked with concern.

"No! I am just thinking... I am just hoping you can be my son." Diego said it emotionally; his eyes tearing up. Asking Daniel this brought back the many memories of his son, Rogelio.

Daniel felt so warm and touched when he heard Diego's request. His eyes turned red. He used both of his hands to hold onto Diego's.

"Mr. Vega. You are my father. Since you saved me from a life of despair in the streets, you have always been my father. I just don't know how to pay you back." Daniel couldn't help crying as he spoke. This reminded him of the Christmas Eve three years ago.

"You know, Daniel, you also saved my life and stopped me from continuing to fall. You also offered me new hope for my life. I just wish... I just wish, you could be my son."

"Mr. Vega. You'll always be my father; the father who gave me a second chance at life on my terms." He moved forward and hugged Diego tightly.

"I want you to become my son legally. I want to adopt you."

Daniel was a little bit shocked by this surprise. If this happened, he would be Diego's legal and lawful inheritor. He was absolutely speechless.

"I will contact my attorney this afternoon and get this started. If you don't mine, I would like to call you Rogelio. You reminded me of my son so much, Daniel."

Daniel just looked at Diego with tears and nodded his head.

That afternoon, Diego contacted his attorney and told him his wish of adoption. The attorney began the lawful procedure to execute the adoption. That afternoon about 4:30, when Daniel was working hard in the warehouse, he was called to the conference room for an urgent meeting. When he walked in, everyone in the room shouted,

"Happy birthday, Daniel!"

Now, he realized that it was not for an urgent meeting. It was a surprise party for his 26th birthday. Later, from other employees, he knew that Diego had planned this surprise party for a week. He didn't know what to say. This was the first time people other than his family in Turda took his birthday seriously enough to celebrate it. He remembered that when he had his birthday before he ran away from home, all he received were sincere and loving hugs from his Dad, Mom, and Grandmother. Life was already so difficult under Communist rule that no one was able to afford a big birthday celebration.

Before he cut the birthday cake, Diego stood up,

"Ladies and gentlemen! As you know, the company has grown stronger and stronger since Daniel joined us three years ago. By now, you have probably become aware that he saved the company from bankruptcy. Here today, I want to formally announce that I have adopted Daniel as my son and legal inheritor. He will take over the company when I formally retire. His Spanish name will be Rogelio Vega."

This surprised everyone. However, they all knew the reason their salary had been increased so much in the last three years was because the company's spectacular growth. This change had been made possible because of Daniel. They were also happy to know the company would have a secure future once Diego retired. Everyone surrounded Daniel and congratulated him. Daniel knew this was a big turning point in his life. Now, he felt he had caught the sun he had been chasing for the past 10 years.

When Daniel returned home, he immediately called his parents about the news. His parents were very happy for him and asked him if he could bring Diego to Romania someday. They enthusiastically wished to meet him.

Second Visit

Again, Christmas approached very quickly. Diego was so anxious to see his sister, Dominga, and her family again. This had been the most joyful time of the year in the last three years. Unfortunately, a week before Christmas, right after dinner, he received a phone call from his sister,

"Diego! I am sorry to tell you that my family won't be able to come this year. My whole family got the flu except me. They've all had temperatures for a couple of days already. The doctors advised us not to travel for a while. In addition, it is contagious, and I don't want them to bring it to your home." She said sadly.

"This is a surprise. I have been waiting for this holiday for a year."

"I'm sorry, Diego!"

"No problem! Just take care of your family and yourself."

When Daniel heard this, he was also very disappointed since he liked them a lot; especially Amato, and Nina. He also felt sorry for Diego since he had been waiting for the arrival of this holiday. Suddenly, he remembered what his mother said four months earlier on the phone, "Why don't you bring Diego to Romania? Your Dad and I would like to meet him and thank him personally." Therefore, he approached Diego,

"Papa! Why don't we spend this Christmas in Romania? My parents would really like to meet you. They had mentioned it several times already."

Diego paused for a couple minutes,

"Maybe it is a good idea. The problem is if we can get the airplane ticket now. It is so close to the Christmas."

"I will contact our travel agent tomorrow and see if he can find some tickets for us." Daniel said.

Next day, Daniel contacted his travel agent from his office about the trip. His agent told him that only first class or business class tickets were available. There was no economy class ticket because those were all sold out. Daniel booked two business tickets. The trip shouldn't be too long. It took only about two and half hours from Madrid to Cluj-Napoca International Airport.

After he had confirmed the tickets, he came to Diego's office,

"Papa! I have booked the tickets, business class. All economy class are booked."

"When will we leave and return?"

"We will leave on December 23rd, Wednesday, and return the 31st, Friday. This way, we will have a couple days of rest since January 1st and 2nd are weekends."

"That means we will leave in four days. That's quick."

"Yes, Papa! We should conclude the business of the year by December 22nd."

December 23rd, they went to the airport via a taxi. Both Diego and Daniel were very busy shopping for some gifts during the last three nights. The airplane arrived nearly half an hour late since there were so many travelers this time of the year. When they arrived at Cluj-Napoca airport, Daniel's parents were there to welcome them. When Daniel and Diego stepped into Arrivals hall, they saw Daniel's parents waiting there for them with flowers. To them, they were more excited to meet Diego than Daniel this time since Diego had changed their whole family's life.

"Hi! Mama! Papa!" Daniel stepped forward and hugged them. Then, he introduced Mr. Vega to them. They offered Vega flowers and Daniel's Mom couldn't help but to hug Diego. Diego felt so warm as if he was part of their family already. He could feel how excited Daniel's parents were. Since Daniel's parents could not speak Spanish or English, all their conversations had to be interpreted through Daniel.

They got a taxi and went straight home. It was only about 10 miles from the airport to Turda. It took them only 35 minutes to arrive home. If it were not for having to pass through downtown of Cluj-Napoca and then drive through a small country road, they would have been home much earlier. Once they arrived, however, Diego realized how bad the living conditions were for Daniel's family. If it were not for Daniel's financial support in the last few years, the family's condition could have been much worse.

Daniel's parents offered Diego the best room they had in the house. Even though, the room was simple and small, it was clean and neat. Gradually, Diego began to comprehend why it was Daniel and many other people were running away to the west to search for hope.

On Christmas Eve, the whole family had a meal together, including Daniel's grandma, his parents, his elder brother, and two sisters, a total of 8 people. Though the meal was not very fancy, it was the best they had to offer. They produced nearly everything on their tiny farm. There were not many greens to eat since it was the wintertime. However, they enjoyed so much the companionship. To Diego, this was a very different feeling from what he had with his sister's family. He had the mixed feeling of being a stranger, but also a family member. He knew this was because it was the first time he met them as well as the language barrier. However, he felt so warmly welcomed by everyone.

On Christmas morning, they opened all of the gifts that both Diego and Daniel brought. They were so happy. Diego also received an antique crystal vase from Daniel's father that had been passed down to Daniel's parents. Though it was not valuable in money, it was imbued with deep appreciation and love. They went back to Madrid on December 31st.

6
HOPE OF FUTURE

On July 10th, 2000, Diego's sister's family moved back to Madrid. Nina just turned 23 and graduated from École Polytechnique in Paris and Amato was 19 and had received admission for Universidad Autónoma de Madrid, one of the best universities in Spain. Her husband, Henry, had resigned from his professor career. They bought a small farm on the north suburb of Madrid. From their new home to Diego's apartment took only 45 minutes. Therefore, Dominga and her family visited Diego often. This had made Diego very happy.

Nina found a job in Madrid as a clothes designer. The place she worked was only about 20 minutes by subway.

One Saturday afternoon at the end of November, she decided to come to visit Diego. Daniel and Diego usually did not work Saturday afternoon. They often stayed late after all employees went home. The business would become very busy since Christmas was coming and they needed to take and distribute the orders. They also needed to make sure there were enough goods for sale this season. Diego was tired and went home around 2:00 PM while Daniel was still checking the inventory they had. When Daniel was done, it was about 3:00 PM. If he went to work or went home with Diego, they usually took a taxi. However, if Daniel traveled alone, he liked to take the subway. To him, taking a taxi just for himself was wasting money.

Halfway from La Almudena station to his home, he came to a street where there were not too many people around. As he came to a corner, he heard a lady's cry and a few guys laughing. When he took a look, he saw there were four guys surrounding Nina, teasing her and making fun of her. They were asking for money. When Nina saw Daniel,

"Daniel, help me." She cried with fear as her body trembled.

"Hey, Brothers. What are you doing? She is my sister." Daniel said loudly.

The biggest and tallest one of the gangsters looked at Daniel,

"Hey! Maybe we can get some money from this guy too." He said.

Daniel realized that they were not retreating, and he did not have enough power to defeat all four of them. He thought of a way to get this situation solved. He still remembered the hand-greeting signal from Primo who was greeting Big Head 8 years ago in Naples.

Without saying a word, he put his right hand up extending his thumb, second finger, and pinky out for a couple seconds and made sure all of them saw it. Then, he quickly changed the hand posture by extending his second finger and thumb pointing at them. The big guy immediately recognized that this was a Milan gangsters' hand sign.

"Hi, a greeting from Primo, brother." Daniel said.

Without saying too much, they waved hands to Daniel and left. After they left, Nina ran into Daniel's chest and hugged him while crying. She was so frightened. She had never been robbed before. She did not know how it was that Daniel could scare them away.

After a couple minutes,

"Let's go home. Hope they don't come back." Daniel said.

Once they entered the busy street, they felt safer. They found a bench beside the street and sat down. Nina's body was still shivering, and she still felt cold. Daniel hugged her tightly for a few minutes and Nina's shivering began to stop. It seemed that she felt safe by being hugged and protected by Daniel.

"How did you scare them away? Daniel." She asked.

"It was a gangster's hand greeting sign from the Milan mafia." Daniel replied.

Nina did not know too much about Daniel's past. She only knew Daniel was a refugee from Romania. She did not know how much he had suffered in the streets for 6 years. To satisfy Nina's curiosity, Daniel took Nina to a coffee shop and found a corner to sit quietly together. They ordered something to drink and Daniel told her of his past up till when he had met Diego.

Nina had never known this. When Daniel talked about the sexual abuse he suffered and then finally having met Diego, he couldn't help his tears. Nina held his hands and kissed them with great compassion. Even though they knew each other for nearly four years, they had never had as deep an emotional feeling as now. They used to treat each other as brother and sister.

Finally, they went home to Diego's place. It was dark and nearly 6 o'clock in the evening when they entered the apartment.

"I was so worried about you, Daniel. I called the company 3 hours ago and nobody answered the phone. What happened?" Diego asked. When he saw Nina was with Daniel, he was very happy.

Daniel explained what happened briefly. He did not want Diego to worry too much. Nina called her Mom and said she would stay at Diego's place for dinner. She would return home Sunday afternoon.

After dinner, Diego was tired and went to bed early. Nina and Daniel went to the living room to chat. She was curious and wanted to know more about Daniel and his life. They chatted till nearly 1:00 AM before they went to sleep. They had never felt so close to each other.

Since it was Sunday, they slept late till nearly 9 AM. After breakfast, Daniel and Nina took a walk in the park. Though Diego did not say anything, he could tell that they liked each other a lot. He was very happy for them. This was probably the best thing to happen to the family. Lunch was late since they had breakfast late that morning. During lunch, Daniel said to Nina,

"I will take you to the station this afternoon." He was afraid Nina was still frightened from what happened the day before. That evening, Daniel was so happy and found it hard to get to sleep. He had never felt this way. He believed that he was in love with Nina.

* * *

Saturday, November 10th, 2000, Daniel and Diego worked very late. This was because Christmas was coming, and they were still behind in arranging everything for the business. They expected it would be a great business year since they had many new products from China, Thailand, and India, of good quality and affordable. It would be one of the most profitable Christmas seasons in the last several years.

When Daniel woke up the next morning, he saw Diego had already gotten up and tried to figure out the shipping schedule for all their customers. He looked tired and stressed.

"Good morning, Papa." Daniel felt a little bit guilty. He believed he should manage all of these schedules instead of Diego. However, he was so tired yesterday and fell deeply asleep.

"I did not want to wake you up this morning. But I saw some conflicts in our schedule. Come here! Let me show you the possible problems we will encounter. Fortunately, I caught it; otherwise, we would have had supply shortage problems for many hot items." Diego explained with excitement.

When Daniel went closer to see the problem, he knew it was his fault since his mind was on Nina for the past two weeks. He needed to see her or talk to her every weekend. He also spent quite some time talking to Nina on the phone. He could not see Nina yesterday and today due to the busy work schedule.

However, Nina came during dinnertime. Nina also missed Daniel very much. In one way, Diego was happy to see the emotional development between Daniel and Nina. However, in the other way, it seemed Daniel did not pay attention to the business as well. Diego needed to pay more attention to the business, especially this time of the year.

After dinner, "Daniel, Nina, I am tired. After my shower, I will go to bed. I need to rest." Diego said and left Daniel and Nina there to clean the dishes. Since it was Sunday, Elena did not work. So, Daniel cooked the dinner.

About 5 minutes after Diego had gone to bed, while cleaning dishes, Daniel and Nina heard a loud thud from upstairs. It seemed like something heavy falling on the floor. Daniel had a very ominous feeling about this and rushed upstairs to see what had happened. He knocked on the bathroom door,

"Papa! Papa! Are you OK?" Daniel asked, but there was no answer. However, he could hear some groaning inside.

Without hesitation, he opened the bathroom. He saw Diego was on the floor and breathing hard. His face was pale. He rushed out of the master bedroom and shouted,

"Nina, call emergency 112. Quick. Your uncle needs an ambulance."

Then, he rushed to Diego and helped him dry his body and made him more comfortable. He knew he should not move Diego till the ambulance paramedics arrived. He just tried to make Diego as comfortable as possible.

Since Diego was naked in the bathroom, after making the call, Nina stayed downstairs to wait for the ambulance. In just five minutes, the ambulance arrived. After they did some emergency first aid procedures and took his vitals, they put Diego on a gurney after covering him up thoroughly to avoid cold exposure and then took him away. Before they left, they gave Daniel the hospital's name and telephone number.

Daniel called Paco. "Paco, this is Daniel. There is an emergency. Mr. Vega just had another heart attack. They took him to the hospital. I need to stay with Mr. Vega tomorrow. Please take care of the business."

He also called Solana about the bad news and asked her to help Paco for the next few days since he did not know the outcome of Diego's emergency treatment. Right after he arranged everything, he and Nina took a taxi to the hospital.

When they arrived, they waited for an hour in the waiting room. A doctor came out to update them and said,

"Mr. Rogelio Vega. Your father is stable now. However, he will need a coronary artery bypass surgery procedure tomorrow. He was lucky to get here on time. Just a few minutes later and the consequences could have been disastrous."

"May I come tomorrow, Doctor?" Daniel asked.

"I would like to come, too, if possible." Nina said.

"I will take one day off tomorrow." She continued.

"Of course, you may come. Just please be aware that the procedure may take a few hours." The Doctor said.

Since there was nothing else they could do, Daniel went back to the apartment while Nina went home with worry and sadness.

The second morning, when Nina and her mother, Dominga, arrived at the hospital, Daniel was already there waiting. Daniel felt so guilty about the whole thing. He blamed himself that Diego's stress was the result of his ignorance of the business. This stress might be the cause that triggered Diego's heart attack.

About 9:00 AM, a nurse came out to tell them that the surgery would begin in a few minutes and she would keep them updated of the surgery's status. Daniel just looked at her with tears and nodded his head.

Time seemed to have passed slowly. They waited and waited without talking too much to each other. Daniel was deep in thought as he traced his experiences back to his childhood, running away from home seeking a new dream, suffering, and finally meeting Diego. He couldn't help that his tears kept flowing. Nina just sat next to him and held his hands. Dominga was able to sense their love for one another. She was happy about it since Daniel was a fine man.

Nearly four hours later, a doctor came out and said,

"Surgery was successful. We have to wait to see over the next few days how he progresses. You may go home now and plan to see him tomorrow afternoon."

The next day, Daniel went to the company to take care of some urgent business and then went to the hospital in the afternoon. When he walked into the recovery room, Dominga was there already. Diego was awake, but quiet. He could not talk too much. It would be too painful for him. He needed to relax and breathe slowly. He just smiled and looked at them. In his mind, he had a lot of thinking to do. Life was just too short and precious.

Around 7:00 PM, Nina, Henry, and Amato came. Nina held Diego's hand next to the bed. She could not help to bend forward to kiss Diego's cheeks. Diego just smiled back. They left the hospital around 8:30 PM since Diego needed rest. He was tired.

Daniel went to see Diego every day after work and reported to him the business conditions so Diego would not worry anymore. Actually, since Daniel had paid more attention to the business in the last few days, everything was on track again. After one week, Daniel took Diego home. Before they left, the Doctor advised,

"You need more rest, no more stressful life, Diego. Whatever you may need to let go of, let it go. Worry and stress are not good for your health condition."

Diego nodded his head in agreement. Actually, he had made the decision that he should retire and let Daniel take over the company. He had confidence that Daniel was able to handle it. Now, he agreed that he should let it go.

After Diego went home, he just did some relaxing exercises as the doctor had recommended. He was just relaxing and allowing Daniel to take care of the business. After Christmas, Daniel told him that, as expected, it was the best and the most profitable season they had ever had. Diego realized that the company could be independent without him now.

On January 2nd, 2001, Diego went to the company and summoned all employees in the conference meeting room,

"I want to thank all of you for your expressed concerns about my health. I also want to thank you for working so hard these last couple of months. This was the most profitable year we had ever had. Solana will distribute extra bonuses for your effort after the meeting." He paused a little bit since everyone was happy and cheerful; especially knowing now they would receive an extra bonus this season. After everyone calmed down, Diego continued,

"I also want to announce an important change in the company. From today, Rogelio will formally take over the company. I am officially retired as of today."

All of the employees had worried about the company's future ever since Diego's health had deteriorated. However, now that they knew Rogelio would take over the company, they were happy. They knew their jobs would be secured.

* * *

After Daniel took over the company, he re-organized some structures, but kept most functions the same as usual. He hired a couple more people since business continued to grow.

Now Diego's life was focused on relaxing. He rested a lot and took things easy. As suggested by the doctor, he also walked in the park one to two hours every day. He was calm and felt more peaceful now. Occasionally, he went to the company just to say hi to everyone.

7
RESCUE CENTERS - SUN SHARING

On March 15th, 2001, during dinner, Daniel said, "Papa, I am thinking of founding a refugee rescue center in Madrid. From our revenue analysis, I believe we will be able to do this successfully without negatively affecting the company. I always wished I could help refugees like me." He looked at Diego anxiously waiting for his opinion.

Diego put his knife and fork down and, looking at Daniel, said,

"Rogelio, it is not a bad idea. You may do what you think is right. Remember, you are the person in charge of the company now." Diego approved his suggestion.

Daniel was hoping to create more opportunities to allow the sun to shine for those refugees like himself. He believed it was time for him to share the sun of his success with others.

On September 1st of 2001, Vega Rescue Center was formally opened in Madrid. This center provided temporary lodging, shower, food, job training and searching, and if possible, immigration services. Once the word spread throughout Madrid, there were more than 100 street people who came to the center's grand opening event for dinner.

Honored guests included: Diego, Dominga, Henry, Nina, and Amato. While they were sitting at the host's table, many refugees came forward to thank them with tears. They just could not believe that there were still good persons in the world with such benevolence. Naturally, they did not know that, in the past, Daniel had been one of them.

When Diego saw the appreciation and happy faces of the refugees, he was deeply moved and very happy. Suddenly, he realized that the real meaning of life was sharing your fortunate experiences with others. He found that this perspective also made his mind more peaceful than ever.

* * *

When this rescue center was reported on TV, a lot of charity money poured in to support its operation. In just 6 months, another rescue center was opened on March 1st, 2002 in Paris. Though this center did not belong to Vega Rescue Center, it was inspired by it. Diego and Daniel were invited as honored guests to the grand opening.

Just in 8 months, Vega Rescue Center had already helped more than 500 people settle down into a productive life. From donations alone, the Vega company actually did not have to bear much of the operational expenses to run the rescue center.

Reunion

On August 15th, 2002, another rescue center, Milan Rescue Center, was opened in Milan, Italy. The Milan Rescue Center was the third non-profit organization that was inspired by Vega Rescue Center. Again, Diego and Daniel were invited to be honored guests. However, because of Diego's heart condition, he needed to stay in Madrid.

To celebrate this grand opening, many people were invited to this event. Other than Daniel, many other important people such as the mayor of Milan, the chief of police department, the bishop, etc. were also invited. There was also a nice dinner for all the street people or refugees. From Daniel's rough estimate, there were probably more than 180 street people that came there for a nice dinner.

At the beginning, the director, Mr. Dante Bruno, first introduced Mr. Rogelio Vega (Daniel) to everyone,

"Ladies and gentlemen! First, I would like to introduce the founder of Vega Rescue Center, Mr. Rogelio Vega to everyone. It was under his dream and influence that this Milan Rescue Center was founded."

After Mr. Bruno spoke for about five minutes, he asked Daniel to say a few words. Daniel stood up and bowed to everyone.

"Ladies and gentlemen. First, I want to congratulate Mr. Bruno for his leadership. Without his leadership, this rescue center would have not been possible. All I wish is everyone in this world have the same kind and generous heart to extend their hands of love to help other unfortunate people. Mr. Bruno has demonstrated his kindness and generosity and this center has provided a good example for others to hopefully emulate. I propose a toast to the success of this rescue center." He lifted up the glass in front of him. Though the drinks they served tonight were either juice or water, the intent and meaning of the gestures were profound.

Daniel did not talk too much since he didn't know Italian well and also didn't know how to give a speech like professional speakers or politicians. After his short speech, almost all of the honored guests, one by one, were invited to say a few words. When all the speeches were finished, dinner was served buffet style.

First, all of the honored guests allowed any hungry street people to pick up their food and return to their table first. After that, there were a couple of volunteers who brought plates of food to the honored guests. During the dinner, as usual, Daniel came down from the stage where the honored guests sat and ate. He went to greet the street people and shake hands with them. He always believed that this would offer them some warmth and feeling of being welcomed. Whenever he participated in these kinds of activities, he was always filled with emotional memories since he was one of them originally. He could easily empathize with them.

When he came to the last table of the second row, he noticed a pair of very familiar eyes staring at him. When he took a closer look at the person, this man immediately bowed his head and turned his head to his left. He was about 50 years old and his face was covered by a beard and mustache. Daniel could not forget this pair of eyes. These eyes were just like his good friend's, Anton Joldea. He remembered that he and another best friend, Jean Aron, always joked with Anton about his eyes in high school. The eyes were very beautiful and charming; able to melt a girl's heart. The eyes that were able to hook a beautiful girl's feeling we used to joke and say as friends.

Daniel woke up from his day dreaming. All these memories had appeared in front of him vividly. The movement of this person was so familiar just like his lost friend Anton. However, when Daniel took a closer look, it was impossible. This man was about in his 50's and his friend, Anton Joldea, should be his age, 28. When this person lifted his head and realized that Daniel was still staring at him, he again bowed his head and turned it to his left. When Daniel saw that, he remembered that Anton was always a shy boy whenever anyone teased him about his beautiful eyes. He always looked down and turned his face to his left.

Amazingly, this man was actually Anton Joldea. When Daniel was in the honored guest area, Anton just thought his face was very familiar, but he had been introduced as Rogelio Vega. He had never imagined that it was really Daniel Eraclid. He believed that Daniel must have encountered the same fate as him by now. The man on the podium was so elegant, educated, and rich. "He was only someone that just looked like Daniel." He thought. However, when Daniel came to his table to meet and greet, he felt so ashamed and embarrassed. After 12 years of searching for the sun, he was still in darkness.

Daniel decided to give this man a test. After he greeted five other people, he looked at who he thought might be Anton again whose head was still bowing down,

"Anton Joldea!" He said in Romanian.

Anton was so shocked to hear someone called his name in Romanian. There was no one who knew his real name; especially not his last name. When he heard this, he looked up and stared at Daniel with big eyes. Now, he was certain that the person in front of him was Daniel. Without saying a word, the tears came to his eyes involuntarily and his body trembled. This was a huge shock to him. He stood up,

"Daniel Eraclid?" He was staring at Daniel and finally uttered these two words.

Daniel was now sure that the person in front of him was his high school best friend that he had been searching for these past five years. He stepped forward and couldn't help but to hug him with tears in his eyes. When he looked at Anton again, he could see all of the 12 years of suffering accumulated on his face. He looked like an old man with wrinkles around his eyes and forehead.

"Anton! Your family was looking for you. They love you."

When Anton heard this, he couldn't help it and began to cry. He missed his home very much, too. However, he didn't want to go back like this, and furthermore, he didn't have enough money to travel anywhere.

"Let's talk more after dinner." Daniel didn't want to talk to Anton too much in public for fear this might cause him feelings of embarrassment. Already, the people around them were curious about what was going on between them.

Right after dinner, Daniel came to the table to find Anton, but he could not find him. He was very shocked and believed that Anton was too embarrassed to see him and left. "No! I must find him. I cannot lose him again." He thought. He began to search for him. When he came out of the dining hall and entered the hallway, he saw Anton was sitting in the corner next to the entrance to the toilets. He was smoking a cigarette butt that he had picked up from the floor. Daniel realized that he didn't run away. He was searching for cigarette butts to smoke. He was addicted to cigarettes. When he saw Daniel, again he bowed his head down,

"Anton! Look at me! Don't be shy with me. We are good friends. Remember?"

When Anton looked up, all you could see was his depressed expression. He felt so sorry for himself. He despised himself greatly. His eyes were vacant and hollow. Daniel brought him to the cigarette machine and bought a pack of cigarettes for him.

"Don't smoke other people's cigarette butt again, Anton. You can get sick." He gave him the cigarettes and joked with Anton as they used to in the past.

Anton took the cigarette and took a cigarette lighter from his pocket. He lighted the cigarette. He inhaled a big mouthful of cigarette smoke deeply and slowly let the smoke out. He felt good.

"This is the best cigarette which I have had in the last two years." Anton began to talk. This had made Daniel very happy.

"But you know, cigarette is not good for you. It can kill you." Daniel joked back.

"I know. But without it, I will die anyway." Anton looked at Daniel with a funny and helpless look.

"Anton! Do you still trust me? Do you still consider me as the best friend you have ever had?"

"Look at me! I am just garbage; human garbage. Why do you still want my friendship?" He looked at Daniel curiously and asked.

"No! Once you are best friends, forever you are best friends, Anton, will you allow your best friend to help you?" Daniel pleaded.

"Why? I will only bring you more trouble and headache. You know, I am hopeless."

"Don't you remember that when we left home on March 15 of 1990 and decided to find the sun, we were filled with hope?"

"Yes! But it was only an illusion. Look at me. I am still in darkness. The sun had given up on me." Anton said and, again, inhaled a mouthful of cigarette.

"But I found it. I want to share this with you. Please allow me to share this sun with you. Remember, we used to share everything. We always joked 'yours is mine and mine is yours.' Remember?" Daniel laughed. Anton looked at him with a smile. Yes! He remembered those happy times together; pure and honest friendship.

"Your parents were missing you very much. Remember, your little sister. The one you like the most. She missed you a lot. When I visited them a few years ago, your little sister couldn't help but have tears in her eyes."

Anton remembered his little sister. When he was 16 years old, his little sister was only 6 years old. She was so cute and followed him everywhere.

"I have missed them a lot, too, in the last 12 years."

"Then! OK! Come with me. As a good friend, let me help you stand up again."

Anton could not help himself and extended his arms and hugged Daniel.

"Let's first go back to my hotel. After you have cleaned up, then we go back to Madrid."

"Madrid! You are living in Madrid?"

"I will tell you all of my story. We have a lot of time."

Daniel grabbed a taxi and went back to his hotel. When they entered the hotel, almost everyone was wondering why this elegant gentleman brought back a sloppy street guy. Anton just kept his head low and followed Daniel to his room.

"First, take a good bath and make yourself clean. Ya! There is a shaving kit there, too, Anton. Shave well and return to your original face." He took him to the bathroom and helped him turn on the warm water.

"Take your time. I will be outside."

When Anton was taking a bath, Daniel made a phone call to Diego.

"Hi! Papa! I have very good news. Remember, I have been searching for my good friend, Anton? I found him in Milan."

"Well! It is very good news, indeed. How did you find him?"

"He was among those people coming for dinner."

"See! When you have a good heart, God will always help you. Bring him home and let's take care of him."

"Yes! Papa! I will not fly back tomorrow. Since Anton does not have an ID card, he could not fly with me to Madrid. Instead, I will take the train with him. It will take us about two days."

"Understand. Everything here is fine. Take your time. I will see you in a couple of days then."

After he hung up the phone, he went to his closet and found some spare underwear, shirts, and pants. He always brought a set of spare ones when he traveled.

When Anton finished cleaning up, he came out of the bathroom. He looked much younger now, though he still felt older than his actual age. He cut his hair short and shaved all of his mustache and beard.

"Wow! You look nice and are still handsome. Come! Change into these clean clothes." Daniel said.

When Anton went into the bathroom to change his underwear, Daniel poured two glasses of red wine. When Anton came out, he gave him one.

"Let's celebrate our reunion. You know! This is will be one of my best days for some time to come." He lifted his glass and proposed a toast.

He then told Anton what had happened to him since they separated in West Germany in 1990. When he was telling his story, Anton could not help but to cry since he had encountered the same situation. The only difference was Daniel found the sun and he didn't. Now, they felt so close together again just like before. During their conversation, it seemed that Anton was somewhat nervous. He kept smoking. They talked until almost midnight.

"Let us sleep now. We need rest. Let me set up a bed on the couch for you. I am sorry that you must sleep on the couch at least tonight." Daniel said.

"Don't worry. It's better than the street. You know."

They set up a nice sleeping area for Anton. They said good night to each other and went to bed.

Around two o'clock in the morning, Daniel was awakened by some noise. He went out to the living room and found Anton was not there. Then, he came into the bathroom and saw Anton was crouched at the corner of the bathroom his entire body was shivering with cold sweat.

"Are you OK!" Daniel was so surprised to see Anton's condition.

"I will be fine." Anton's tears came out helplessly.

Daniel could see now that Anton was also addicted to drugs. Anton was experiencing withdrawal symptoms. Daniel saw this happening often when he was part of New Heaven. He didn't know what to do. All he could do was to wipe the sweat off him and pour him some warm water. After a couple hours later, it seemed that Anton felt better. His body's trembling had stopped. He was more relaxed. He gave him a hug and encouraged him to take a shower and then go to sleep.

When Anton was taking a shower, Daniel came to the living room. Now, he knew he had to face another huge challenge, to help Anton overcome his addiction to drugs. He knew it was not going to be easy, but for his best friend, he would try anything. He entered into deep thought. When Anton came out of the bathroom, Daniel was still in the living room. It was nearly 4 o'clock in the morning.

"Come here! Anton! Lie down and relax."

Anton looked at him. He was so tired and felt restless. He lay down on the temporary bed.

"Face down! Anton."

He turned his body over. Daniel began to massage his shoulders, back, and finally legs. At beginning, Anton felt very uneasy since Daniel treated him so nice. However, after only 20 minutes or so, he fell sleep. Daniel stopped his massage and went into his room and fell asleep as well. They slept until nearly 9:30 AM. When Daniel woke up, he saw Anton was still sleeping. He looked at him and began to think of Anton's past and his own past. He felt sorry for himself, but even more sorry for Anton. He made a decision that it didn't matter how or what, he would bring back Anton from the dark side of the world. He went to the bathroom and took a shower.

He called the train station from his room to reserve two tickets from Milan to Madrid. First, they had to take the Salvador Dali from Milan to Barcelona, a 13-hour train ride. Then, they had one hour of rest and again took the Renfe from Barcelona to Madrid which was another 5-hours-and-14-minute train ride. It would be a long and exhausting trip. When he came out, he saw Anton was already waking up. He was sitting there as if frozen and his eyes didn't blink. He was in deep thought.

"Hi! Did you sleep well! Anton!"

Anton looked at Daniel with wondering expression, "I am sorry about last night."

"Don't worry about it. You must be in great pain when it happens."

"Do you think I still have hope? I don't know what to do. Daniel. I want to get rid of it, but I can't. I wished I had drugs last night. I am glad that I didn't, and you were with me. This was the first time I was able to resist it, you know."

"How did it happen?"

"From our conversation yesterday, I knew you had encountered exactly the same situations as I had. However, there was a big difference. I stayed in the gangster's group until I was kicked out and you ran away to continue your searching for the sun."

'How were you kicked out?"

"After I traveled in West Germany, Austria, Netherlands, France, and finally here in Milan for 5 years, in order to survive, I was absorbed into Milan's local gangster group. I was only 21 years old, young and good-looking. I was used as a sexual tool to make money for the family."

"Did you belong to the group led by Primo? You know he had two loyal followers, Dante and Nino." Daniel still could not forget these three Milan gangsters who abused him when he was 19 years old.

"No! They have the territories of central and the east side of Milan. My group was in the west side. I heard that Primo was killed in a gun fight about three years ago."

"Then, what happened to you?"

"Three years ago, when I was 25 years old, I began to get addicted. One of my long-term customers always gave me that and enjoyed it with me. In just 8 months, I couldn't live without it. I was dumped because I couldn't bring more money into the family than I spent for drugs and medicine. I was forced out."

"You have been on the street for three years?"

"In order to get some money to support my addiction, I stole money or even robbed people on the street. I begged for food and before you know it, I was in hell."

"Do you want to change yourself? Anton! I need this answer. Only if you are willing and have a strong will to change, can I help you." Daniel looked at him with a gentle, but serious look on his face.

Anton looked down and said, "I have always wanted to. I have tried it by myself several times for the last three years. I failed. It is not easy, you know, Daniel! It is just like there is a devil inside of your body. You cannot control it."

"OK! The first thing after we arrive in Madrid, I will take you to a drug rehabilitation center. You must keep your promise as you used to with me. Remember, we trusted each other without masks. Can we do the same?"

Anton nodded his head. Anton had run out of the cigarettes that Daniel bought for him. He was feeling uneasy. Daniel knew that he was craving for cigarettes. However, there were none there. Furthermore, he wanted Anton to also quit smoking. He continued his talking on purpose.

"When you feel better, I want you to work for me. You can then be independent. I know that it will not be easy for you. However, whenever you are depressed, just think of your family, think of your suffering and think of the dream you had. You are only 28 and still have your whole life in front of you."

After breakfast, Daniel took Anton out to shop for some clothes and shoes. He also took him to a barbershop to have his hair cut neatly. After all of these were done, Anton felt like he was a new man. He must start from the beginning. He must appreciate what he has received now and decide not to make any more mistakes. "I have felt the warmth of the sun, I cannot lose it again. I must chase it." He felt these emotions and thoughts sincerely.

They took the 9:10 PM train from Milan to Barcelona. The train would not arrive in Barcelona until 10 AM the next day. That night in the sleeper car of the train, Anton's withdrawal symptoms started again around 2 AM. Daniel spent the time with him and wiped his sweat. When he saw Anton's pale face and shivering body, he knew that Anton had so much pain inside. He wished he could help him more. It was not until 3:30 AM when Anton began to feel better.

When they arrived in Barcelona, they had about a one-hour break before taking the next train to Madrid. The train would leave at 11:20 AM. Daniel took Anton to a restaurant near the train station and had some food. After eating, they had some espresso. When they were in the restaurant, Anton kept looking at those customers who were smoking. Daniel knew that Anton was struggling with his cravings.

"Do you need one? Anton."

"Yes! I do. But I think I shouldn't."

When they were going out of the restaurant, Daniel took Anton to a convenience store next to the restaurant. He bought a pack of cigarettes and also two packs of chewing gum.

"Try to resist it. Smoke only if you fail in controlling it. I heard chewing gum could help you stop smoking. Why don't you try?"

Anton felt both appreciation and embarrassment, but he trusted his best friend, Daniel was only trying to help and did not judge him for being addicted. He took both the cigarettes and chewing gum. He took one chewing gum out from the pack and put into his mouth and began chewing it. The flavor was sweet, and the chewing provided a distraction from his craving for the moment. They went back to the train station and got ready to take off. It would be another 5 hours of travel on the train. Anton kept chewing his gum and tried not to think about cigarettes while they were on the train. Finally, he spoke to Daniel and said,

"Daniel, do me a favor. Please keep this pack of cigarettes for me. If I need it, I will ask you. This way, I won't be tempted easily."

Daniel smiled at him. He knew that Anton wanted very much to quit. He would need a lot of encouragement and friendship now to be successful. Daniel took the cigarettes and put them in his jacket. The train arrived in Madrid at 4:30 PM. They took a taxi back home. Since Diego already knew Anton would return with Daniel, he had already asked the maid, Elena, to prepare the guest room for Anton. When they arrived home, it was 5:30 PM already. Daniel used his key to open the door to the apartment and led Anton to the living room. He knew that Elena would be busy cooking dinner now and Mr. Vega would be in the living room either watching TV or handling some company business.

"Papa! This is Anton. My best friend who I mentioned to you several times."

Anton bowed to Mr. Vega politely and at the same time, feeling embarrassment. He was always shy, even now as a 28-year-old adult. When Mr. Vega looked at him, Anton reminded him of Daniel. "Another unfortunate sun chaser. I am so glad that Daniel found him." He thought.

"Anton! Treat this place as your home. If you need anything, just tell me or Rogelio." Since Diego adopted Daniel as his son, he always called him Rogelio.

Then, Diego asked Anton about his story. Since Anton could not speak Spanish, Daniel had to be the interpreter. Basically, Anton had nearly the same encounters as Daniel. The only big differences were Daniel found his sun and Anton didn't and also Anton had become addicted to drugs and cigarettes. During the conversation, Diego could see that Anton tried to hold back his emotions. Diego knew that Anton would need a lot of help and love at this time. Around 7:30 PM, Elena came and told everyone that dinner was ready.

"Rogelio! Can you wash the dishes for me? I need to go now. My daughter has a cold."

"No problem, Elena. Please, go and take care of your daughter. I hope she gets better soon."

Elena took her belongings and left. For six years, Daniel had always treated Elena as his cooking and Spanish teacher. He had learned so much about cooking from her. Though there was at least a 25 year difference in age between them, they were just like good friends. During the dinner, Daniel said,

"Anton! As you promised, I will arrange for you to see the doctor in the drug rehabilitation center tomorrow."

Next morning, Daniel searched for a Madrid drug rehabilitation center. He found there was one called Madrid Positivo that was founded by Dr. Jorge Gutierrez. It seemed they had the best rehabilitation program. He took Anton to Madrid Positivo the next day and registered him. They told Daniel that they would like to keep Anton there for a few months and see his progress. They also told Daniel that, in general, the successful rate for rehabilitation was not high, only 14 to 20% depending on each individual. They also mentioned that those who were successful usually had a strong will and also had a lot of support and love from family and friends. The following few months were the most critical for Anton's treatment. When he left,

"Daniel! I am afraid. I am afraid that I cannot handle it." He couldn't help to hug Daniel with tears.

"I will be here to see you every day, Anton. Just think about your suffering in the last 12 years, think about your family, and think about me. You can't fail this time. You must face it, otherwise you will lose your sun again." "I'll come to see you tomorrow." Daniel left.

Daniel often went to see Anton and stayed with him, encouraged him, and expressed concern for his feelings. When Dr. Mendoza told Daniel about Anton's progress, he couldn't believe that Anton had so much progress in just three months. Daniel knew that Anton had felt his sun that was shining on him and was prepared to only move forward to be his best self.

One morning, when Daniel and Diego were eating breakfast, Daniel received a phone call,

"Hello, Mr. Vega. I am sorry to tell you that Anton was very sick last night. He threw up and had some diarrhea. He also had a high fever. I wonder if you are able to be here to watch him and keep him company. We are short of manpower now." Dr. Mendoza said.

"Thank you, Dr. Mendoza. I will see if I am able to find someone to be there with Anton. You know, it is the end of month and it's inventory time for the business. I will be extremely busy and cannot be there all the time. But I will find someone to go there." Daniel replied.

From the telephone conversation, Diego understood the situation for Anton.

"Rogelio. I know you will be very busy today and tomorrow. I can go spend time with Anton, but I think I need to be at the company if there is any big decision needed to be made though." Diego said.

"Papa, actually, it is true that we will need you at the company. It is the most important time of the month. Furthermore, it is near the end of the year. If we don't order more supplies now, it would be too late for Christmas." Daniel explained.

When they were talking, Elena was serving their breakfast and knew the situation.

"Mr. Vega, let me ask my daughter, Belicia, if she can go take care of Anton. She is available now since she is switching jobs and has one week off. Let me call her and see if she would like to do it?' Elena said. Belicia, who was 26 years old, was the only daughter Elena had before her divorce ten years ago.

"Really? That would be great, Elena. I really appreciate it; especially in this urgent time." Daniel said.

"No problem, Mr. Vega." She replied and went to pick up the phone and called her daughter. A few minutes later,

"Mr. Vega. Belicia will be very happy to go. She is bored at home. I told her the place and she will go there directly." Elena said.

* * *

When Belicia arrived at the rehabilitation center, she reported to the check-in desk, and then she was led to Anton's room. Anton was removed from his regular quarters to this special care room. Anton's fever was still high, and he was in a deep sleep.

"Please use this ice towel to cover his forehead occasionally. This will help his temperature drop." The nurse said and gave Belicia a towel and a bucket of ice water.

Belicia nodded her head with a smile. After the nurse left the room, she began to use the ice towel to cool down Anton's forehead. After 30 minutes, Belicia could not help but to take a detailed look at Anton's face. From her Mom, she roughly knew Anton's past and condition, but they had never met each other. This was the first time that Belicia saw Anton and so close. She discovered Anton still had his shy and boyish look, though his face was pale. She could feel the suffering that Anton had experienced for the past twelve years. She sincerely felt sorry for him and was filled with compassion.

Half an hour later, Anton woke up and saw Belicia. At first, he thought it was the nurse, but from how she was dressed, he realized that she was not. He looked at Belicia curiously and wondered who she was and why she was there.

"I am Belicia. My Mom works for Mr. Vega. Mr. Vega cannot come to look after you, so I volunteered to come." Belicia said.

Anton looked at this young and beautiful girl. He was somewhat excited, and it seemed he had recovered from his sickness to a certain level. He was tired but could not help asking Belicia questions with his poor Spanish. When he was sleepy again, Belicia just encouraged him to close his eyes and sleep.

About 9 PM, Daniel and Diego came. They saw Belicia was tired and fell asleep on the couch in the room. When they stepped in just for a moment, the nurse came in to take and record Anton's temperature and pressure. Belicia woke up from the couch,

"Hi, Mr. Vega." She had been there for nearly 9 hours.

"Thank you, Belicia. You are very kind." When Diego handed her a 20,000 pesetas bill (about US$150) (140 pesetas = US$1).

"No! No! Mr. Vega. You don't have to pay me. I am very happy to do it." Belicia refused to take the money.

Anton woke up as the nurse was taking his temperature.

"His temperature has dropped. If we can keep it down, he will be well on his way to a full recovery." The nurse looked at Belicia, Diego, and Daniel with a smile. It seems she implied that because of Belicia's care, Anton had recovered more quickly.

When Anton saw everyone and heard their conversation, he could not help that his eyes became watery. He had never been treated so nicely and kindly in the last twelve years. He just looked at them with appreciation. He swore that he would never fail in his rehabilitation. He must be strong and stand up independently; especially now that the sunbeam was shining on him.

Anton recovered rapidly. In just two days, he moved back to his regular room. It was no surprise that, other than Daniel, Belicia came to see and talk with Anton almost every day for a week. When they were together alone, they felt so comfortable and the gap between them got closer and closer each time they met. Anton had never had this kind of feeling.

"I need to begin my work tomorrow. But I will come to visit you whenever I can, OK?" Belicia said to Anton.

"I will miss you every day. Come to see me more often. Dr. Mendoza said, if my condition continues to improve, I might be released at the beginning of next year." Anton said with excitement. He deeply believed and was confident that he could conquer himself; especially with Belicia's encouragement and support.

Christmas time had approached. Daniel asked Dr. Mendoza if he could take Anton out from the center to have him enjoy a few days of holiday with them. Anton had been at the rehabilitation center for four and half months now and had had great improvement. Dr. Mendoza granted Daniel's request.

On Christmas Eve of 2001, it was a great reunion. In the dining table, other than Diego, Daniel, and Diego's sister's family, Anton, Elena and Belicia were also invited. This was a rare situation. Both Elena and Belicia were guests, but also served food to everyone. They talked and laughed. In order to participate in this dinner, Elena and Belicia went to South Spain to see their family a week before.

Dr. Mendoza told Anton that he should go back on January 2nd. Anton and Belicia took this opportunity to go to the movies and walked in the park when the weather was nice. Otherwise, they would stay at the mall. They just wanted to be alone together. They had enjoyed each other very much. They were deeply in love. "Strange destiny." Anton said to himself. He was pulled by an angel from hell to heaven. Just only six months ago, he was still in the streets.

January 2nd, Anton returned to the rehabilitation center. This was the first time Anton was free from rehabilitation. He was completely free from drug addiction. One month later, Dr. Mendoza told Daniel to pick up Anton. His rehabilitation was a success. He was a new man now.

On February 1st, 2002, Anton was picked up by Daniel and went back to Vega's home. Anton was placed in guest room temporarily. That evening at dinnertime, Daniel asked, "Anton, I wonder if you would like to work for the Vega Trading Company? I have already acquired Mr. Vega's approval. Our warehouse has increased to double its size. We need an extra person to handle the inventory. Though the job is very basic, it is also very important to the company's success. Once you are familiar with the company's business, you will be promoted."

Anton knew that Daniel said this because he didn't want to hurt his feelings. He acknowledged in his soul that Daniel had already given him a chance at a second life. He must appreciate it and love himself from now on. When he thought of this, he couldn't help it and extended his both hands out to hold Daniel's hands.

"Daniel! Thank you very much. You are my sun. I have found my sun." He said with tears.

"That's great. I will ask the company's attorney to apply for an ID card for you, so you can work legally. Now, you have a job. I think you should write home. Your parents have worried about you for so many years. Let's take a photo in the warehouse, the place you will work, and send it to your parents." Daniel said. He encouraged Anton to write a letter to his parents. He didn't want to tell them before since Anton was still unwell. He believed that only when Anton was able to stand up by himself, should he then contact his parents.

Next morning, Daniel took Anton to the Vega Trading company with his car. After he introduced Anton to everyone, he took him to the warehouse. He explained to Anton that it was his first legal job in Spain, too. Daniel took a photo of Anton. They also got a shot together.

Daniel also hired a personal tutor to teach Anton Spanish and English. He also taught Anton how to run business according to what he learned both in school and from Diego as well as from his own personal experience.

When Anton's parents received the letter, they were so surprised and excited. They thought Anton had probably died since they had not received any message from him for so many years. In addition to the letter, they also saw his photo in the warehouse and another with

Daniel. Now, they knew that they were not in a dream. It was real that Anton had found his sun, his future. Anton's Mom couldn't stop weeping.

A couple of weeks later, Anton received a letter back from his father. When he opened it, his hands were trembling. He couldn't believe that he was able to have a connection with his family again.

At the end of the month, Anton received his first salary, 130,000 pesetas (US$900). He was so excited and sent half of it home since he still lived at Vega's home. He also included a photo of himself with Belicia. When his Mom received the money and photo, she couldn't help but to cry. She missed Anton so much.

Anton kept saving money whenever he could. He also planned to move out of Mr. Vega's home so he could be more independent. However, the most desire he had was visiting his family in Romania. At the beginning of December, after working for 11 months, he had saved nearly 900,000 pesetas, the equivalent of US$6,000. The first thing he wished to do was go home to visit his family that he had not seen for 12 years. One day, he was walking in the park with Belicia, and said,

"I plan to visit my family in Romania during Christmas vacation period. I am wondering if you would like to come with me? My family would be very happy to meet you." Anton asked.

"I would love to, Anton. We have known each other for more than one year now. I believe it is about time to meet your parents."

Anton was so excited and purchased airplane tickets for Belicia and him. He also told Daniel and Mr. Vega about his plan. They thought it was the right time for his visit since he had a steady job and a good girl friend.

When Anton and Belicia arrived at Cluj-Napoca airport December 23rd of 2002, his whole family was there to welcome him. They hired two taxis because, including his grandparents, parents, and his sister, total there were 7 people.

Anton's family couldn't believe that Anton was really coming home, especially his grandparents and parents. They loved him so much since he was the only boy at home. They stayed till January 1st of 2003. During this period, Anton's family had a chance to know Belicia and had a great time. Anton also took Belicia to visit Jean. From Daniel, he knew Jean had returned home after the first year. They were all grown up now, not the same as when they were 16 years old. They had to face reality. Fantasies or illusions were not in their minds anymore. They did not talk too much about the past 11 years.

The following March, Anton moved out of Diego's home and rented an apartment near the company. It took only 15 minutes to walk from his apartment to work. Now, he had his privacy and freedom. Belicia often visited him during weekends and stayed till Sunday nights.

***

New Family

On October 5th, 2002, after more than two years of being in love, Daniel and Nina got engaged. This was a big event in both the Vega's and Daniel's families. One year later, they got married on October 4th, 2003.

First, the wedding was held in Madrid and Daniel's families in Romania were all invited. Daniel's grandma was so excited; especially because this was the first time she flew in an airplane. Actually, none of Daniel's family had taken an airplane before. It was a great experience even though it was a short flight. Naturally, all of Vega's employees were invited and many of Diego's friends as well.

After the wedding, Daniel and his wife Nina returned to Romania with the families since there were still many relatives that couldn't come to Madrid for the wedding. It was another big celebration. Diego did not go since it would be another tiring trip. He stayed in Madrid.

Daniel and Nina could not stay too long in Romania. After a short honeymoon in Switzerland, they returned to Madrid. Daniel was now the key person for the company; especially with Christmas coming soon. It would be another busy season for the Vega Trading Company.

December 20th, 2003, Nina was pregnant. This had brought more great news and joy for the whole family. Diego had been very quiet since October's wedding. In his quiet contemplations, he sincerely thanked God's mercy and kindness.

On Christmas Eve morning, Daniel woke up early as usual. He looked at Nina still sleeping like the fabled sleeping beauty. He also thought of their future child who would be born the following July, and Daniel smiled.

Daniel went to his study and looked at the T-shirt on the wall that had been with him for the past 12 years. This T-shirt reminded him of the suffering and the joy of the past. This T-shirt also had given him great inspiration and encouragement. He thought of a proverb that the Chinese said: "There is a will, there is a success."

On Christmas Eve, he came to the street where he and Diego met the first time. Life was strange and mysterious. He believed he was one of the lucky ones who had received so much from heaven.

8
FAREWELL

January 1st of 2004, the whole family got together. Diego, Dominga, Henry, Nina, Amato, and Daniel were gathered in the evening. This was under request of Diego to have a family reunion on this New Year day. It was rare that the weather was nice and warm this time of year. After a great dinner,

"There is something I have been wanting to say for the last few years. I have realized that I am a lucky man. I have all of you to be part of my life and memory. I really appreciate all of you. Life is strange, but if you treat it nicely and carefully, life will also take care of you." Diego gave a five-minute speech and talked about his life, marriage, his wife, son, sister, niece and nephew, all of them brought him a good memory. Finally, he said,

"The most important person whom I appreciate most in the last 8 years is Rogelio Vega. It was a strange destiny. Without him, my last seven years would have been the darkest days of my life. However, he gave me the sun that has been shining my life. I am so glad I met him." His eyes turned red and looked at Daniel. Daniel looked back at him with tears. He knew that though Diego had changed his life, Diego's life also was changed. This night, it seemed that Diego had some feeling that he couldn't explain. He must say these words to all of them.

He looked at Nina, "I am so happy to see both you and Rogelio love each other. The new life is coming and that is the hope and joy." He looked at Nina's stomach with a peaceful and satisfied smile.

"I am happy and satisfied about my life. I cannot ask for more. I just want to say these things to you all tonight." Diego lifted his wine glass and proposed a toast.

The night lasted until midnight with cheerful celebration.

The following morning, January 2nd, 2004, Daniel was waiting for Diego to wake up so they could take a walk as they did occasionally. When Daniel waited till 10 AM, he knew that Diego might have some difficulty since all of them went to bed after midnight. Usually, Diego woke up before 7 AM.

He came to Diego's room and knocked on the door, but there was no answer. He opened the door and saw Diego was still in bed. However, when Daniel took a closer look, he realized that Diego had passed away in his sleep. His face was peaceful and smiling. Diego was 73 years old.

ABOUT THE AUTHORS

Dr. Yang, Jwing-Ming

Dr. Yang, Jwing-Ming was born on August 11, 1946, in Xinzhu Xian (新竹縣), Taiwan (台灣), Republic of China (中華民國). He started his wushu (武術) (gongfu or kung fu, 功夫) training at the age of fifteen under Shaolin White Crane (Shaolin Bai He, 少林白鶴) Master Cheng, Gin-Gsao (曾金灶). Master Cheng originally learned taizuquan (太祖拳) from his grandfather when he was a child. When Master Cheng was fifteen years old, he started learning White Crane from Master Jin, Shao-Feng (金紹峰) and followed him for twenty-three years until Master Jin's death.

In thirteen years of study (1961–1974) under Master Cheng, Dr. Yang became an expert in the White Crane style of Chinese martial arts, which includes both the use of bare hands and various weapons, such as saber, staff, spear, trident, two short rods, and many others. With the same master, he also studied White Crane qigong (白鶴氣功), qin na or chin na (擒拿), tui na (推拿), and dian xue massages (點穴按摩) and herbal treatment.

At sixteen, Dr. Yang began the study of Yang-style taijiquan (楊氏太極拳) under Master Kao Tao (高濤). He later continued his study of taijiquan under Master Li, Mao-Ching (李茂清). Master Li learned his taijiquan from the well-known Master Han, Ching-Tang (韓慶堂). From this further practice, Dr. Yang was able to master the taiji bare-hand sequence, pushing hands, the two-man fighting sequence, taiji sword, taiji saber, and taiji qigong.

When Dr. Yang was eighteen years old, he entered Tamkang College (淡江學院) in Taipei Xian to study physics. In college, he began the study of traditional Shaolin Long Fist (Changquan or Chang Chuan, 長拳) with Master Li, Mao-Ching at the Tamkang College Guoshu Club (淡江國術社), 1964–1968, and eventually became an assistant instructor under Master Li. In 1971 he completed his MS degree in physics at the National Taiwan University (台灣大學) and then served in the Chinese Air Force from 1971 to 1972. In the service, Dr. Yang taught physics at the Junior Academy of the Chinese Air Force (空軍幼校) while also teaching wushu. After being honorably discharged in 1972, he returned to Tamkang College to teach physics and resumed study under Master Li, Mao-Ching. From Master Li, Dr. Yang learned Northern-style Wushu, which includes bare-hand and kicking techniques as well as numerous weapons.

In 1974 Dr. Yang came to the United States to study mechanical engineering at Purdue University. At the request of a few students, Dr. Yang began to teach gongfu (kung fu), which resulted in the establishment of the Purdue University Chinese Kung Fu Research Club in the spring of 1975. While at Purdue, Dr. Yang also taught college-credit courses in taijiquan. In May 1978, he was awarded a PhD in mechanical engineering by Purdue.

In 1980 Dr. Yang moved to Houston to work for Texas Instruments. While in Houston, he founded Yang's Shaolin Kung Fu Academy, which was eventually taken over by his disciple, Mr. Jeffery Bolt, after Dr. Yang moved to Boston in 1982. Dr. Yang founded Yang's Martial Arts Academy in Boston on October 1, 1982.

In January 1984, he gave up his engineering career to devote more time to research, writing, and teaching. In March 1986, he purchased property in the Jamaica Plain area of Boston to be used as the headquarters of the new organization, Yang's Martial Arts Association (YMAA). The organization expanded to become a division of Yang's Oriental Arts Association, Inc. (YOAA).

In 2008 Dr. Yang began the nonprofit YMAA California Retreat Center. This training facility in rural California is where selected students enroll in a five-year to ten-year residency to learn Chinese martial arts.

Dr. Yang has been involved in traditional Chinese wushu since 1961, studying Shaolin White Crane (Bai He), Shaolin Long Fist (Changquan), and taijiquan under several different masters. He has taught for more than forty-six years: seven years in Taiwan, five years at Purdue University, two years in Houston, twenty-six years in Boston, and more than eight years at the YMAA California Retreat Center. He has taught seminars all over the world, sharing his knowledge of Chinese martial arts and qigong in Argentina, Austria, Barbados, Botswana, Belgium, Bermuda, Brazil, Canada, China, Chile, England, Egypt, France, Germany, Hungary, Iceland, Ireland, Italy, Latvia, Mexico, the Netherlands, New Zealand, Poland, Portugal, Saudi Arabia, South Africa, Spain, Switzerland, and Venezuela.

Since 1986 YMAA has become an international organization, which currently includes more than fifty schools located in Argentina, Belgium, Canada, Chile, France, Hungary, Iran, Ireland, Italy, New Zealand, Poland, Portugal, South Africa, Sweden, the United Kingdom, the United States, and Venezuela.

Many of Dr. Yang's books and videos have been translated into other languages, such as French, Italian, Spanish, Polish, Czech, Bulgarian, Russian, German, and Hungarian.

For more books by Dr. Yang, Jwing-Ming please go to the YMAA Publishing website.
https://ymaa.com/publishing

Dr. Yang, Jwing-Ming

Dr. Robert J. Woodbine

Dr. Robert J. Woodbine was born in New York and raised in Colon, Panama as well as the South Bronx and Harlem. He graduated from the prestigious Hotchkiss School and attended Harvard University until he left his junior year to work for General Motors on the assembly line in Framingham, Massachusetts to support his family.

As a result of the oil embargo of 1974, he was laid off, but eventually found his way to Xerox Corporation and Digital Equipment Corporation where he worked in professional sales and marketing for a combined twelve years. During that time, he earned his B.Sc. in Management and Organizational Behavior from Lesley College in Cambridge, MA.

At the age of 41, he left corporate and enrolled as a full-time student at the National College of Naturopathic Medicine in Portland, OR where he earned his doctorate of Naturopathic Medicine (ND). He subsequently completed his master's degree in acupuncture and Oriental medicine (M.Ac.O.M.) at the Oregon College of Oriental Medicine, also in Portland, OR.

His love of creative writing and expression was sparked by a book of poetry written by LeRoi Jones given to him by his father. Writers Don L. Lee, E.E. Cummings, Robert Ruff, and Sonia Sanchez were also sources of inspiration. He spent one year as a member of the Countee Cullen Writer's Workshop with Sonia Sanchez at the Schomberg Library in Harlem writing and performing.

As a retired naturopathic doctor and acupuncturist, Dr. Woodbine is currently immersed in the study of Taijiquan and Qigong with Dr. Yang, Jwing-Ming whom he's known since 2001. As a creative writer and wellness educator, he is interested in sharing that which will inspire others to be self-reliant mentally, emotionally, physically, and spiritually to uplift the human experience. Toward that end, he continues to write and perform his poetry and explores the healing power of sound through playing the didgeridoo, throat singing (which he learned from Fabian Maman, David Hykes, Rollin Rachelle, Nestor Kornblum, and Sayam Bapa of Huun-Huur-Tu), and Quartz crystal bowls. Currently, he is writing his memoirs, a book on Black men's health, and co-authoring a book on Qigong. He is the proud father of two sons and four grandchildren.

Dr. Robert J. Woodbine

www.ingramcontent.com/pod-product-compliance
Lightning Source LLC
Chambersburg PA
CBHW050945120626
46552CB00001B/385